Deuce's Exile

Clark Family Legend, Book 5
By
Richard E Friesen

1
SUICIDE MISSION

Earth Colony: Angel's Planet
Thurman Colony Year 289
Burgundy Lee's Freelance Diary

Alone and free, I still needed a job. A starship had to have fuel and rent on the docking berth, even here on Planeta De Angel. While I could sleep on the ship, I needed food. It had been three weeks since my last paying gig, and that hadn't been a good one. I sauntered into town one more time, pretending to be a cocky pilot.

I had gotten away from bastards who wanted to control my life, who had created me to be some hero ace, but I'd left behind my friends and family, not to mention any idea who I was, to do it. I could starve on my very own.

My hollow stomach weighed down my heart as I walked alone, bitter, and lost, but still free, through the arched passage that ran from the spaceport to Puerto Fronterizo, the first dome on Planeta de Angel. Today, between the windows, the walkway walls had what looked like Mayan artwork. Some windows looked out the sides at the spaceport and the mountains beyond. The other windows angled up, which allowed for watching starships coming and going through the roiling sulfur-soaked atmosphere.

Landing here was a bit of a challenge, but that was why so many frontier pilots like me came here, not to mention the people that hired us. The cloud cover and the active volcanism kept Council of Planets police and other officials, not to mention most tourists, away.

When the walkway ended and I emerged into the domed town called Puerto Fronterizo, the magnitude of Angel's hubris struck me. The dome sat on a mesa, above an ocean on one side and a river of lava on the other. Where the two met, vast steam rose into the heavens. We lived in a soap bubble, perched between horrors, as precarious as my identity.

A grav-bus left from the shuttle port, heading to Volcan Diablo or Extranjera, the only other settlements. I'd never been to either, but rumor had it the mines there produced gems and minerals beyond compare, but also in small quantities by galactic standards.

Off to the left, up against the dome, one of the giant printers rested, waiting for a new building to print. With one technique, and limited building materials, all the buildings had charcoal gray walls with blue and orange highlights. The expensive places had those colored bits arranged into patterns or highlighting the doorways.

I strolled past shops, plasma pistol on my hip, which no one gave a second look. The tech shop had a show going on its outside wall, advertising the latest cleaning robots. A grav-car went by overhead, settling on a roof in the next block. Not many people bothered with those here.

Marta, a dark-haired matron, leaned out of her counter window. "Hey, Deuce! Want some empanadas? They're hot today!"

Laughing, I waved. "Too hot for me. Be back later."

What I really wanted was someone to call me Burgundy Lee, but that name was dangerous to bandy about. It would make it easier for the bastards who created me to find me. Being the freezer of Brandeis Clark, the most famous pilot in human space, just sucked, but if I wasn't her second coming, who was I?

Three doors down, I stepped through a dark entryway into the Abogada. I turned right then left and then the saloon expanded before me. With brighter lights than any tavern I'd ever been in, the three-meter bar lay on the left, and a little hall on the right ended in the bathrooms, but had four simulators, two on each side. The place smelled of whiskey with undertones of sweat, but not stale beer.

In the other corner, at the end of the bar, a door led to a back room, used for various forms of business. The far wall had six booths, all empty, and the rest of the floor had computer-capable tables, with printed plastic chairs. The seven other patrons in the room, pilots all, occupied three tables.

Tall, dark-haired Ramon, the bartender, nodded to me, poured a margarita, and set it on the bar. "Hola, Deuce."

No one here, perhaps no one on the entire planet, used their real names.

One of the guys beckoned me. He was called Bomber, I assumed related somehow to his old-fashioned leather bomber jacket. He had black hair and black eyes with a flat nose, and was a decent pilot, but not as good as anyone in my squadron back at Clark Academy. "Hey, Deuce! Come look at this one."

At the table with him was a woman with ash-blonde hair and an ethereal air who went by Winsome. She could outfly Bomber. The funny thing was that most times being a freelancer didn't require a good pilot, just a daring one.

That Bomber wanted to show me a job meant it was one these two didn't want. What freelancer would turn down a job? Some jobs were too hot, like if the Council of Planets Navy would be involved. Some pilots had scruples, others didn't, but we all had lines we wouldn't cross.

I sauntered over to the table and cocked my head. "Does this one scare you too much, Bomber?"

Winsome, lithe, graceful, and always smelling of cookies, also the only woman besides me in the bar, snorted. "This one's even too crazy for you, Deuce."

I turned a chair around and straddled it, since impressions and acting tough and cocky seemed to matter in places like this. Then I took a sip of my margarita and set the glass on the table. "So, what is this absurd job?"

Bomber gave me a shrug, feigning nonchalance as he sipped his beer before answering. "Nothing big, just a blockade run."

He punched something up on the computer. Two carriers, two battleships, and dozens of fighters and destroyers appeared, orbiting a planet which seemed to have an icecap on the equator.

I leaned closer, my combat tactics classes from the Academy kicking in to analyze the formations. The battleships were facing outward, and the destroyers, in their orbits, maintained outward firing lines. That blockade was designed to keep people out rather than keep people in. Falling out with any velocity at all and decelerating into the atmosphere would leave a ship in the crosshairs for minutes. If one had to decelerate at fallout, which all ships did. At least so far.

The thought made me smile. I'd been telling my former boss at Pauley Spaceways that we could fix that little problem of fallout velocity, and prevent the feedback from blowing up the reactor, but his bosses wanted to work on multiple drive systems to make faster ships instead. The question was whether I could fix the fallout velocity problem by myself, or almost by myself. I had a good mechanic here, which would help.

I wasn't about to let any other freelancers know that, though. I waved my hand through the hologram, dismissing the blockade with a grunt. "Suicide mission."

Winsome took a pull on her beer then scowled. "Which means it doesn't matter how much money they're offering."

I licked some salt off my margarita glass and took a sip. "Not even a little bit."

Of course, the money mattered. Everything out here was a risk versus reward calculation. Winsome's comment made me think a lot was being offered, but it had to be enough to float a starship or keep one afloat. The risk was insane.

Why did I think I could do it?

I gave a nod toward the back. "Hey, Bomber, want to try to beat me in the simulator again?"

Bomber rose, taking his beer with him. "You bet."

I followed, and over at the simulators, poured my drink into a tumbler with a lid. Drinking and flying was dubious, but fun.

Later, after several simulated flights, first where I waxed Bomber and then when Winsome joined us for some team flying, I walked out of the simulators to find a stranger drinking at the bar.

I nodded in that direction. "Is that the guy with the suicide mission?"

Winsome and Bomber both indicated it was.

I sighed and rolled my eyes. "I guess he's going to talk to me, no matter what."

Taking my drink over, I went and sat in one of the booths. There, I got out my computer and reviewed my finances and my readiness for a job. By the time the stranger made it over, I'd gotten thoroughly depressed. I had to get a job, or leave, since I couldn't pay for my berth. But I had exactly zero places to go.

I could go back home. My parents would take me in. I could get the job at Pauley Spaceways back, submit to the bastards who'd created me, submit to being Brandy part two. But if not Brandy part two, then who would I be?

A stranger slipped into the booth across from me. He had thick, wavy hair, as dark as his eyes that shone black with hope. His tailored shirt and silk ascot were absurdly out of place in the Abogada, in the entire dome, but the money they spoke of enticed and comforted me.

He offered his hand. "I am Ghazi."

When I shook his hand, he had a firm grip, and I caught a whiff of saffron. How strange. "Deuce."

If he weren't offering a suicide mission, I would have been ready to accept right away.

Ghazi laid his other hand on mine and looked in my eyes as if trying to read my thoughts. "Ms. Deuce, a pilot I need, and desperately."

I pulled my hand free and laid it on the table. "I've heard a little. What is the job, exactly?"

Ghazi glanced surreptitiously around, dubious. "Perhaps we should go to a more secure location."

That got me to raise an eyebrow. I was dealing with an Angel's planet novice. Oh, joy. Had the others taken him into the back room? No wonder Bomber had a model of the blockade. "This is the most secure place in the dome. Nothing and no one are what they seem on Planeta de Angel. If it looks secure, it probably isn't."

With a quick glare over at Bomber, Ghazi blew out a big breath. He did skip the recriminations-part and went straight for business. "It is simple. A passenger there is to retrieve from a planet and revert said passenger to Earth."

Deceptively simple, and incomplete. "And where said passenger lives, there just happens to be a blockade of warships. Whose warships?"

I had an idea, but I wanted him to say it.

Ghazi smiled like a used tech salesman. I'd hoped for more. "Should that said blockade exist, it is likely to be Nova Roma."

That, of course, created more questions. Nova Roma had been admitted to the Council of Planets after the war where my sister Brandy had become the legendary ace. But since the day the Romans had helped against the star sharks at New Serengeti, there had not even been a hint of war. Why, then, were the Romans blockading this planet? Why did getting someone to Earth matter?

I jabbed my finger into the table to emphasize each word, shaking my glass. "What would the Romans gain by such a blockade?"

Ghazi shook his head, glancing down at the table. "This I do not know."

A lie. In other words, as a mere pilot, I had no need to know. The second question might be phrased as a demand. I put my fingers on my lips for a moment, as if considering. "For so dangerous a mission, I would need a million credits, plus expenses."

Ghazi jerked back, eyes widening. He recovered himself quickly. "That is a high price. How much are these expenses?"

He hadn't said no. Exactly how desperate was he? "Five hundred thousand." I raised a hand as Ghazi started to answer, then leaned against the booth back, trying to look casual. "I need half of that up front for modifications to my ship. And if the modifications fail, the mission is cancelled, but I keep the two-fifty. The other two-fifty you send before I leave."

Ghazi leaned forward, waggling a finger at me. "How do I know you will not simply take the two-fifty and leave?"

He should just trust me, obviously. Holding his gaze, I picked up my margarita and sipped it. "Put it in an account. I'll give you the bills and receipts. Some will be for berthing fees and food, and an hourly rate for me and my mechanic." I grabbed my computer and flicked a couple bills to him. "Those are a start."

He checked his computer and scratched his head. "For this price, we could get a decent ship of our own."

I snorted and set my cup down on the table hard enough he could hear the clunk. "First, you don't need a decent ship, you need a great one, or an armada. Second, who would fly it?"

That they were hiring a freelance pilot said they didn't have the stomach for any official action. Afraid of a war, no doubt. With me flying the mission, if I failed, the Romans wouldn't know a damn thing about who had hired me. The stakes were a lot higher than getting mineral rights or registering a habitable planet.

What was I getting myself into?

Ghazi started to lever himself out of the booth, but I raised my hand. "Keep looking for a pilot. Pretend I turned you down."

He raised an eyebrow at me then smacked the table. "Why did you waste my time?" He stomped out of the Abogada, shaking his head.

I wandered to the bar for a fresh drink, winking at Ramon, and then went back over to Winsome and Bomber, both of whom were a bit tipsy by then.

Bomber brought up the blockade on the table projector and played random approaches, watching the blockade ships win every time. "Did you steal that job out from under me?"

I gave him a sidelong glance and sipped my margarita. "You *said* you turned it down. I was just leading him on to see if I could get berth money from him."

Winsome snorted.

Bomber groaned. "I should have thought of that!"

An hour later, I wandered out of the Abogada. On the way back to the spaceport, I stopped to get empanadas at Marta's. A younger woman served me while Marta herself cleaned tables in the back. The aroma of spicy fried meat and baking bread wafted out from the kitchen.

I bit into a chorizo and cheese empanada with a flaky crust. With my mouth full, I nodded to Marta. "I met a guy, a stranger, who said he knew your cousin José."

Marta came over, cleaning rag in hand. "Ah, sí? What did he say?"

Of course, Marta had no cousin José. I shrugged. "Just that he knew José. He's a well-dressed man with dark hair. I met him at the Abogada a little earlier."

Nodding, Marta snapped her rag at an imaginary crumb on the counter. "I will check with José and see what he knows."

I bought another empanada and headed back for the space port, walking out beneath the mural vault. This job excited me, more than any I'd taken on. If I succeeded, I'd be doing something no human had ever done.

I stopped in my tracks. Here I was flying impossible missions, changing the assumptions on what could be done, just like my sister. Well, damn. The problem was, I really wanted to do it, especially since Pauley Spaceways, and all the other engineers, thought it couldn't be done. I couldn't avoid being a little like my sister, but I just wanted to find who Burgundy was.

2
IN PIECES ON THE GROUND

On the walk from Puerto Fronterizo to the space port, past the mural walkway, now showing the caldera of a volcano from inside, I came to the main terminal building. There, shops sold black market and smuggled goods right out in the open for anyone to buy. I recalled how uncomfortable I'd been at seeing the Shark's Den in Launching City Spaceport on Thurman as I left for Solomon Tech as a teenager. The one here with its gaping maw and shimmering brown and green outer wall seemed tame, flanked by a brothel designed to look like an island getaway, complete with an ocean breeze blowing into the terminal and a shop selling hallucinogens and other chemical entertainment.

I'd been lucky to survive my first weeks here, in this strange place. Now, I strode through the main terminal and into the private berth area, a maze of landing pads and docking tubes that had grown almost organically. I turned left past the Lava Grill, right at the Diamond Berths, a quick jaunt over the chasm, and down into the Basin, right again at José's Star Parts, and out near the Precipice.

There, in Berth P19, *Hiram's Revenge* waited. I touched the window next to the inner air lock. At my palm print, it cleared so I could see my ship, black and menacing on the docking pad. I paused to consider my home in the lonesome stars. When I wasn't flying, it reminded me that no one waited for me anywhere. I went on past, the window darkening again as I left.

Today I had business farther out. After four more turns and going through docking area R, I arrived at a door, the last door. On my right, a set of windows overlooking the Precipice, three hundred meters down to a steaming lake, separated by sharp rock ridges on both sides from lava flows. To the left, beyond that door, a building extended out over the drop. It looked like it might fall in at any moment, but I'd learned better. A starship could land there, and it wouldn't fall.

On the door, painted—not digital, not a screen, but painted—in non-descript letters, was *Earl Cristo, Starship Mechanic.* I rang the bell. He had a doorbell.

From inside a dog went *Woof* and the door unlocked. Well, sort of a dog.

I stepped inside the foyer, a spotless room with smooth gray surfaces, a counter, and a door to the back, not even a single chair or computer.

A medium-sized, four-legged robot dog bounded over and sniffed at my feet. I had no idea if it could smell or not, but it clearly thought it could, and that it was a dog. I did wonder what kind of weapons Earl had installed.

I bent down, and like always, wondered if I should pet him. "Hello, Robberre. Where's Earl?"

Roberre looked back into the other room and whuffed.

Earl Cristo, tall and handsome with blond highlights in his black hair, walked in from the shop floor, wiping his hands on a smart towel, which pulled the grime from his skin into its warp and weft.

He stopped at the door to the front room, leaning on the jamb and looking delicious. "Hello, Deuce. How flies the *Revenge*?"

"Hi, Earl. The *Revenge* is flying just fine, when I have a job. This time, I need something special. Have some time?"

I had worked with him in a couple instances, adding smuggling bays to the *Revenge* and enhancing the radar, but he had a reputation among the freelancers: if you wanted something special, you went to Earl Cristo. I just wished he had a personality.

"Always. Do you have the money?" Earl asked.

I cocked my head, wondering if I might crack Earl's ironclad shell. "How about we go to the Lava Grill and talk about it over dinner?"

"I have already eaten."

My heart sank. I just wanted to eat with a friend. "No problem. Expenses up front, make bills coming up to a hundred fifty thousand or so. Double that if it works."

Earl rubbed his chin. "That will pay for some special work. What would you like done?"

I leaned up against the counter and smiled. "How about we change how flying in Lu space works?"

Earl didn't even react to that pronouncement. Maybe he was the computer, not Robere. "Very well. Bring the *Revenge* over in the morning and let me know what you want me to do."

I reached out and shook his hand. "Part of this money is to keep anything we come up with secret. We can negotiate partial ownership, too."

Earl paused to think. "Of course. Twenty percent will be adequate."

"Done."

I turned, walked out of Earl's place and all the way back through the winding spaceport to the Lava Grill, by myself. There I bought supper—pulled pork with Carolina mustard sauce and coleslaw—and headed to the *Revenge*.

When I got to berth P19, the airlock door unlocked after it scanned my retina. I pulled the heavy door open and stepped through. It swung shut behind me with a clunk.

The other port-side airlock door, with an automatic air pressure sensor, stood open. With no place particular to be, I strolled out of the airlock and up the docking tube, a flexible tunnel suspended from above, but with a stiff floor. It took me right to my upper deck airlock, which let me in with facial recognition and the presence of my control bracer. I'd paid extra for the remote-control package and the bracer, but it let me do almost anything with the *Revenge*, except fly it, without being on the bridge.

I walked in through the airlock doors, caressing my black beauty. The room in the back had many uses—lounge, dining area, gym, and more, each with retractable furniture. Now, it had an exercise bike and weight machine folded out of the ceiling. There was also a low bar about thirty centimeters off the ground.

On a whim, I jumped and landed in a handstand on the bar. It felt good to move my body once in a while, just because I could.

From that position, I watched the airlock door close behind me. To the right, a floor-hatch led to the ladder and down to the cargo deck, but it was closed for now, leaving only the personnel deck to live in, which was sufficient.

Pushing off with my arms, I flipped forward, landing in the corridor that ran up the center of the ship. Ahead, past the two bunk rooms on the right, the head, and the galley on the left, lay my sanctuary: the bridge. On the way there, I powered on the engines using my bracer.

When I stepped onto the bridge, I relaxed. It was my place, with my imaginary Hiram in the copilot's seat. I'd left the real Hiram behind so that I could escape the bastards who created me. Would it have been worth giving in and becoming what they wanted to keep Hiram? I doubted they would have let me stay with him, and it was far too late now.

The shielded glass canopy over the bridge angled down from the wall at the back to the floor at the front, though I never used that canopy to see anything. I used Virtual Vision instead. If I had joysticks there, I could fly the ship from my bunk.

Two seats, both sunk into the floor and both with twin 3D joysticks, waited for me.

Climbing into the pilot's seat on the left, I put supper into the little storage bin next to the seat, which could keep things warm or cool. Then I grabbed my helmet from the copilot's seat and put it on. I'd left it plugged in. It saved me two seconds when taking off.

As soon as my Virtual Vision erased the ship so I could see in all directions, I typed my launch request into the computer and got a course back from space port control. I disconnected the docking tube and waited until it folded back into the terminal building. Then I pushed my right foot down to increase main thrust. *Hiram's Revenge* lifted off dead slow. I wanted to get away from all these people who were not my friends, almost as much as I'd wanted to get away from the bastards who created me. Somehow, I was more alone down on the planet than out in space.

At last, I cleared the mountain range and incoming traffic, rising above the volcanic ash and sulfur clouds. I lit out at a full four gs, acceleration pressing me down into my seat. A few minutes later, the sky faded from magenta to black. I checked where all the planets were on my navigation computer then plotted a course system inward and a little left of the sun.

A Jovian orbited there, almost like a binary star.

I hit the button to jump to Lu space. The stars stretched and faded, turning into strange amorphous colors for three seconds. Then the computer dropped me out again, colors stretching into a plume of light and heat. When it dissipated, I was back in normal space. The stars reappeared, and off to my left sat the hot roiling planet called Granchico. Beyond, the system's star roiled almost as much, solar flares rising high, as if trying to immolate the gas giant.

I sat in my pilot's seat and watched while I ate my pork. Out here, alone in my ship, I recalled how I'd felt flying away from Thurman, my home planet, that last time, how I'd escaped. The freedom had been so sweet. It still was.

I enjoyed the solitude for an hour or so. Then I went back to my bunk and slept the night away.

In the morning, I flew out of the hold the star had on my ship and jumped back to Angel's planet. On the way down, I let Earl know I was coming and then realized I was still paying for my docking berth. It would be at least days figuring this out in Earl's shop.

As I dropped through the atmosphere, I sent a message to the spaceport and canceled the berth. I would get a new one later if I needed it.

By the time I got through the volcanic turbulence and down to the spaceport, Earl had the floor of his place open. I brought the *Revenge* down over the Precipice and moved under the cantilevered portion of Earl's shop. There, a wind blew outward, keeping the toxic atmosphere at bay.

I tipped the *Revenge's* nose upward and moved her in. As soon as the nose pierced the level of the shop floor, a guidance image appeared in my Virtual Vision. It showed the *Revenge* and the shop so I could land the ship just where Earl wanted.

When the aft section in the model cleared the outside wall, I leveled the *Revenge* out again by bringing the rear upward. I moved forward to the blinking dot on the floor, extended my landing skids, and set the *Revenge* down.

The large, rectangular shop floor had room for a second ship the same size as *Hiram's Revenge*, but I assumed we would be alone for this. On the left, just past where the floor tipped down to open the shop, the heavy door leading to the lobby sat closed. Beyond that was another closed, unlabeled door. The two doors on the other side both stood open. One seemed to lead to a room for spare parts of all sorts, the other to a fabrication shop with a medium-sized 3D printer and other equipment like saws, grinders, and drill presses. It reminded me of the Pauley Spaceways fabrication hangars back on Thurman, though this was smaller and a lot of the equipment less new.

The floor over the Precipice closed, and Earl walked out to meet me. I lowered the ramp on the cargo bay and shut everything down. Taking off my helmet and putting it on Hiram's seat meant I was on the hard ground again and not free of gravity.

I needed this job, though, and if the modifications worked, I would have a ship like no other, so I unbuckled, got up, and walked down the short corridor to the common room, still laid out as a gym.

There, I opened the hatch and climbed down to the cargo deck. The ladder angled out since the cargo deck was wider than the personnel deck. The cargo space didn't amount to much. In the corner on the other side of the ramp from the ladder was an engineering station. There were access hatches to get to the reactors and gravity drives below, some food storage and smuggling bays along the walls, and hooks for cargo straps. The walls, hatches and all, comprised the sealed inner hull for the *Revenge's* double-hull design.

The cargo ramp descended from about a third of the way across the floor. I didn't bother going around, hopping over the edge instead. Earl waited at the bottom with Roberre.

The metal dog sniffed my feet. "Woof."

Earl rubbed his hands on his smart cloth again. "Hello, Deuce. Please show me what you want done."

I got out my pad and connected it to Earl's public network. Then I swiped an old simulation up on the wall. I'd modified it in my spare time when I worked at Pauley Spaceways. I'd had time to do things like that since I'd been trying to save money for a ship and didn't have a social life.

A simple ship with visible gravity force lines moved across the wall. Then the gravity forces changed, forming a point anomaly that sent the ship into Lu space.

I pointed at what looked like a continuous climb away from real space. "Right now, all ships accelerate through Lu space at the same angle they entered it. That means, they continue to get farther from real space and their exit velocity gets faster. The light plume gets bigger, too. I need to precisely control both."

At the end, the simulated ship dropped out of Lu space, almost straight down.

Taking the simulation back to the beginning, I added my modifications. "I figure, to stay in Lu space we need to keep the forward momentum, especially since moving is the point. But we should be able to reduce the upward vector of the thrust. Like this."

On the wall, the ship went up into Lu space through the anomaly, but halfway through, it started coming down again. Thus, when it came out of Lu space, the drop was tiny compared to the first one.

Earl frowned. "In order to change that vector without changing main thrust, you would need to tri-modulate the field."

I glanced over at the simulation again as it repeated on the wall. "Exactly. We also need to deal with the feedback from the gravity drives to the reactors. I figure increase the gauge on the wiring and increase the strength of the magnetic bottle on the fusion reactor, but what we really need is a power coupling or something that won't let the surge get back to the reactor in the first place."

Earl nodded once, seeming to take up all the room in the hangar. "I will do all of those. How are you going to fly a tri-modulated field?"

He was just going to casually do what engineers had been attempting for close to forty years? Right. I guess I would see soon enough. He had nailed the other issue; a bi-modulated field required both hands and both feet. I could just grow a third hand to control a tri-modulated field, but that seemed like a lot of work.

I looked up into the cargo hold, imagining the controls on the bridge. "You do the power coupling and any hardware required to tri-modulate the field. I'll work on the controls, and we'll meet somewhere in the software to make it all work."

Earl leaned in and followed my gaze up into the ship. "Since I will be taking *Hiram's Revenge* apart anyway, I could rig the cockpit so you can easily make changes. We will connect it to building power so you can run simulations with the actual controls."

I didn't want the *Revenge* torn apart. "You don't have a simulator?"

Earl shook his head and gestured at his shop. "I have no need."

Valid point. He wasn't a pilot, and I certainly didn't want to run these simulations at any place I could rent anywhere on Angel's Planet.

I put my hands on my hips and frowned, not wanting to tear *Hiram's Revenge* apart. It felt like dismantling Hiram. I didn't have a damned choice, not if I wanted this damned job. "Good idea, then. Let's get started."

Turning, I walked back up the ramp. By disassembling the cargo bay, we could get access to nearly everything on the ship. While Earl gathered tools, I opened the access panels for the drives and the reactors, air seals popping when I did. Roberre trotted up the ramp with a toolbox on his back, and we set to work in earnest.

Four hours later, with the *Revenge's* guts showing and cargo bay deck and wall plating stacked at the bottom of the ramp, I straightened up and stretched my arms overhead. Stepping on structural beams to get to the remaining intact floor, I made my way back to the ramp while Earl stood in one of the holes, bent over tracing wires or something.

My stomach growled. "Hey, Earl, want to go get something to eat?"

He straightened up and looked over at me. "No, thank you. I wish to continue working. I will start on the bridge while you are gone."

As I walked out of the big hangar, through the lobby and out into the spaceport maze, I wondered if the man ever ate. The walk through the spaceport to the tunnel with its images of molten rock and rising smoke, and into Puerto Fronterizo seemed infinite. I just wanted someone to talk to.

Instead, I talked to myself. "Oh, Hiram, if only you could have followed."

We would have made a good team out here, but I'd checked on him a while back. He'd married a woman named Hannah. They had two kids and he was teaching at Solomon Tech. I wondered if he ever thought of me.

Eventually, stomach still complaining, I made it to Marta's Place. I went to the counter and ordered four empanadas and a horchata to drink. Then I sat at one of the three tables to eat and wait.

I'd begun to feel a little better by the time Marta emerged from the kitchen, wiping her hand on a towel. Just seeing her improved my mood, though she was a business acquaintance, no more a friend than Earl.

She sat down across from me. "Hello, Deuce. Have I shown you the most recent pictures of my granddaughter back on Earth?"

Marta pulled out her pad and brought up the pictures. She showed me photos of a family celebrating a toddler's third birthday in their backyard. The mom looked a bit like Marta, and everyone appeared happy playing on the grass and eating cake in the shade of a tall tree. I wondered how long it had taken these pictures to get here. They could be a year old, given the irregular flights out this way.

We talked as if we were family friends for half an hour. I made up my own family back on New Zion, where my grandfather ran a place that rented recreational airplanes.

At last Marta got around to Cousin Julio. "I did track down that friend of Julio's you met." She swiped at some crumbs on the table. "Did you know that boy is a genuine Greenwood Planet lawyer? Got some real money too, though he's kind of mum about his job, like it's some top-secret government spy thing or he's just ashamed of who he works for."

A Greenwood lawyer with money. They were supposed to be the best. Not a surprise, but on retainer for the government? What government and why? The biggest thing was he didn't seem to have come looking for me, and I thought I'd kept my real name secret. I had. If he had been looking specifically for me, he'd done it quite subtly. Of course, now I was planning a flight only I could pull off. Oh, joy. But I had to get *some* job. What job did *I* want?

I forced a chuckle and lifted an empanada as if in toast. "Your cousin does meet the most interesting people."

Marta reached out and patted my hand. "Well, I'd better get back to the grind. Enjoy your empanadas, Dear."

She rose and went back to the kitchen, leaving a void where her warm presence had been.

I wolfed down the last of my empanadas, left a gigantic tip, and headed over to the Abogada. I even managed to saunter like a cocky pilot the dozen meters or so over to the bar.

After walking through the dark entry and around the corner into the lighted bar, I stopped on the threshold and checked out the room. Winsome and a pilot I didn't know sat with potential customers in booths on the edges, but no one sat at the tables around the floor. It would get busier later.

With no pilots to trade lies with, I went and sat at the bar.

Ramon got me a margarita and set it in front of me. "Hola, Deuce. Cómo estas?"

I raised my glass and snorted. "Taking risks."

A slow grin came to his face as he held glasses upside-down over the sonic cleaner. "Is that not a freelancer's job?"

I gave him a wink, sipped the cool drink with a hint of salt, then nodded toward the booths. "Any good jobs?"

Ramon wrinkled his nose. "One you'd be lucky to see any money, the other is hot. Depends on your risk level, I guess."

Hot would mean a criminal, or at least someone who'd run afoul of a government somewhere. If the man had money, and the *Revenge* wasn't sitting on in pieces in Earl's shop, I would at least think about a job like that. Maybe I should have waited, but I *wanted* to upgrade the *Revenge*.

I took another sip of my margarita, savoring the salt and lime. Then I shook my head for show. "What did you think of that guy with the suicide mission yesterday?"

He set some tortilla chips on the counter, with salsa. "Mi amiga. You are joking with me. He has backers, with money, true, but one must be alive to spend such money."

I raised my glass to him. "This is true."

I hadn't paid that much attention to what Ramon might know before. In the future, I would. He might even get an arrangement like I had with Marta.

Grateful for the information, and the confirmation, I asked Ramon about his family.

An hour later, having nursed that one drink, and having been educated about Ramon's husband and daughter, I tipped him very well and headed out.

When I reached the door and stepped out beneath the dome, Winsome caught up with me. "Hey, Deuce."

What did she want? She appeared to have left a potential fare sitting in the bar.

I lifted my chin in greeting, then nodded back toward the bar. "Hey. Not a good job?"

She scowled. "He was a putz. No way he could pay for more than a liner ticket."

We walked on past Marta's Place and into the tunnel heading back to the spaceport, where now images of roiling purple clouds showed below a sunny peak of gray rock.

Winsome's hand brushed mine. "Would you be interested in maybe a partnership?"

I stopped in the middle of the tunnel and faced her. "What kind of jobs need two ships?"

Pedestrians scooted around us as Winsome ducked her head. "Maybe not that kind of partnership, or maybe just for now." She leaned in and kissed me. No tongue, but on the lips. When she pulled back, she took my hand. "At least for tonight."

A little warmth and togetherness, skin touching skin, would be nice. Really nice. But I was not attracted to Winsome, and this kind of broke the unspoken rule about independent freelancers. Then again, maybe that was an illusion. I just had no desire to get naked with Winsome. I suspected when it was over, I would feel more alone anyway, like I had the few times with Jason Samuels, my coworker at Pauley Spaceways.

I hugged her and whispered in her ear. "That is the sweetest offer I've had in years. I'm just…"

"Into guys." She pulled away but looked at her feet. "I'm sorry. I just thought…sorry."

Winsome started to walk farther into the spaceport, even though I was going the same direction.

I hurried after her, dodging more foot traffic. "Let me buy you a cookie. We can talk."

Winsome laughed. "A cookie?" Then she gave me a sidelong look. "I'd like that."

We went to the Lava Grill with its orange and red décor and a cook in back sweating over a hot grill. There we bought cookies and iced tea.

We sat down at a table with a picture of Krakatoa on the top, and I grinned at her. "You're from New Zion?"

She looked up, startled. "Um, how did you know that?"

One single word, putz and it was a guess. I shrugged. "I went to Solomon Tech."

That got us talking about parents and friends, where we'd come from. I didn't ask and didn't offer how I'd gotten here. Nor did I mention my famous freezer twin. Winsome had secrets, too, but talk of childhood memories avoided most of them.

When we rose to leave, Winsome touched my arm and gave me a self-deprecating smile. "Thank you, Deuce. You make me want you more."

I waved that off. "Ha. Only because I can wax you in the simulator."

She went off left, and I stood a moment, feeling alone. That was the closest thing I'd had to a talk with a friend since escaping Thurman. Sighing, I headed back through the winding passages to Earl's. When I got there, I knocked and walked into the lobby.

Roberre trotted over to the inner door that led to the shop. He squatted down, front legs out. "Woof!" Then he turned and trotted away. Five meters into the shop, he stopped and looked over his shoulder, like a dog wanting me to follow.

I followed.

The *Revenge* still sat where I'd parked it, but Earl stood up on the top, raising the bridge canopy off with a gravity lift. Using a remote, he guided the shielded glass up and away from the ship.

A scream built in my throat. My refuge was coming apart. I reached out to find a wall, anything solid to hold onto. With a stumble, I caught the door frame.

"Earl will put it back together," I told myself while trying to catch my breath. "It will go back together. It will."

Roberre stopped by the ramp up into the cargo hold and looked back at me. "Woof!"

"Yeah, yeah, I'm coming."

I pushed off the door and walked over, in no hurry to see what Earl had done to my ship. Inexorably, I made it up the ramp where I had to step carefully around holes in the floor. Two large cables ran up the ramp toward the front of the ship. One went down into the guts, toward the fusion reactor. The other ran up underneath the bridge.

I climbed the ship's ladder—more of a steep stair—to the main deck. In the common room, I stopped. The air felt different.

I got to the bridge as Earl, standing out over the bow now, finished guiding the canopy to the shop floor. He'd also removed the panels beside the pilot's seat, exposing the joystick mechanisms, and one by the pedals in case I needed to do something there.

The engineer in me was fascinated by the workings. I knew all the theories behind each part. I knew how it worked, and I wanted to dig into it. Maybe that curiosity could keep down the irrational terror that it would never go back together churning my guts.

Clenching my stomach muscles and my teeth to keep the scream in, I assisted Earl getting the bridge ready so I could make changes to it and run it as a simulator, not connected to the ship's reactor.

That night I lay in bed in my quarters on *Hiram's Revenge* reciting the mantra to myself. It will go back together. It will go back together. It will go back together.

3
CHANGING THE RULES

Two weeks later, I ripped off my flight helmet and threw it into Hiram's seat on the *Revenge's* dismantled bridge. I had just simulated a fall-out low over a planet with a blockade for the twentieth time. Assuming the pilots and gunners in the blockade were paying attention, I would die.

I'd tried every combination of a third joystick and third pedal trying to make flying a tri-modulated field work. Extra left joystick, extra right joystick, even one between my legs, and in every case, the half second it took to release the extra one and get my hand back on the regular joystick was a half second where the enemy could take aim and fire.

Now, it was possible I would surprise them enough that a half-second wouldn't matter, but I couldn't count on incompetence. Even with the changes, I anticipated there would be a plume of light and heat, and the blockade ships would fire on an unexpected fallout. Moreover, my drives would be down for fallout, so how fast I could get going again mattered.

A woof came from below, so I got up and stepped to the edge of the bridge. Earl emerged from the fabrication shop carrying a piece of equipment about half the size of me. It had a plasteel cylinder, the kind that would hold a magnetic bottle connected with two short cables to a metal box that had a little screen on top, but gave no clue as to its purpose. Out of the metal box ran another stiff power cable with a quantum coupler.

He'd gotten ahead of me.

I put my hands on my hips. "Is that the power coupling?"

Earl stopped and looked up. "It is. It tests well in the lab. Are you ready to test it in the *Revenge*?"

The terror I'd been keeping down clogged my throat. That made me angry. I was going to have the hottest ship in this corner of the galaxy. I was.

I turned to head back through the ship. From the common room, I climbed down the ladder and met Earl in the dismantled cargo area. "Let's get it hooked up."

The quiescent fusion reactor sat forward, beneath the floor. Earl carried the coupler there and set it on a beam. The barrel-shaped reactor had feeds in from the hydrogen tanks, but Earl had already disconnected the old power cable leading out. I looked again; the new cable was a larger gauge.

Earl wedged his large body into the space beside the fusion reactor, leaving room for the power coupling. He tossed up a hand grav-lift, which I caught.

He nodded to the power coupling then pointed to where the fusion reactor main power cable connected. "Please lower that here."

I attached the lift to the coupling with the adhesive pads and turned it on. The power coupling came off the floor as a tiny gravity field formed around it. I maneuvered it over to the opening in the floor and lowered it down.

Earl turned it around until a lone cable was toward the fusion reactor. Earl slid the cable-end against the fusion reactor and triggered the quantum coupler, which sucked the assembly against the reactor and created a locked seal, merging wires together.

On the other end, he connected the power coupling itself to the gravity drive with its quantum coupler, fastening the plasteel cylinder to the Revenge's frame nearby. Then he pressed a button on top and the little screen lit up.

Earl patted his power coupling. "All set. Should we test it?

I gestured toward the gravity drive. "What about tri-modulating the field?"

"Ah." From a pocket, Earl produced a small, mirrored device that curved back in on itself. "It turns out most of that is software, and this, a new neutrino-graviton modulator."

He leaned over and opened a panel on the gravity drive. Then he pulled a screwdriver from another pocket and reached in to remove the existing modulator. The one he pulled out had a less complex curve and was a little smaller.

Earl installed the new modulator, straightened up, and scratched his head. "How are the controls coming?"

I threw my hands up. "Awful! No combination of pedals and joysticks works, even if I switch a joystick function."

Earl furrowed his brow. "Do most ships not use the computer to control jumps these days?"

"I can, certainly, but this..."

I'd been about to say that going into combat I needed to make fast decisions which couldn't be programmed. The computer *could* modulate the field. And the computer could take voice commands, plus I wouldn't need to do anything with the tri-modulation after fallout. Using the computer with voice added would give me three ways to control the ship, one for each modulation vector.

Leaning over, I kissed Earl on the top of his head. "Get this thing buttoned up! I have software to write. Then we'll test the whole thing in space."

★★★★★

Two days later, I flew *Hiram's Revenge* out of the roiling atmosphere of Angel's Planet. Earl sat next to me in Hiram's seat. The Virtual Vision provided by my helmet erased the ship's bulk, including all but a shadow of Earl, which let me concentrate on flying.

I accelerated upward, away from the planet at an ordinary pace. Soon enough, we cleared local traffic. Not long after that, the jump light came on, I hit the button. The stars stretched and faded to those weird coruscating colors as always.

Then we waited. We had to get a little way into Lu space before our new trick mattered.

Asking Earl if he was ready seemed redundant. And if his coupler didn't work, we'd blow the reactor and die anyway.

I took a deep breath and committed. "Tri-modulate. Decrease vertical vector one half g."

The computer beeped in my ear. The vector graph changed. Reactor temperature stayed rock-solid. A word appeared in my heads-up display, *Boost.*

"What's this boost?"

Earl answered, his disembodied voice sounding as flat as always, "The power coupler has a capacitor. That should give you a gravity boost, if needed."

I hit the fall-out button. "You mean I can get more than four gs?"

The weight came off my body. The colors stretched and brightened. A light plume erupted around the *Revenge.* The stars reappeared.

Earl spread his hands. "For a short period of time."

I started plotting the next jump, the harder one. "How did our return to normal space look?"

Earl fiddled with the ship's computer. "The light plume was eighteen-point-one percent less than expected for a jump of that duration and exit velocity forty-three percent less."

That required some processing, but it made sense. The light plume didn't go down as much as the velocity because the plume included energy generated from forward thrust, too.

I flipped us over and started back toward the solar system, and one icy ball of rock called Amante Helada. The green course line appeared in my Virtual Vision. I moved my finger to the jump button as I waited for the light to come on. The enormity of what I was about to try dawned on me. From light minutes away, I needed to fall out within a hundred kilometers of an atmosphere, closer if possible.

After thinking about it, I adjusted the course to skim the planet. And I gave the computer the entire process ahead of time—jump, tri-modulate, reduce vertical thrust, fall-out. It occurred to me that I could also increase vertical thrust, but I couldn't think why I would want to.

When the computer had the new course, I hit the jump button. The stars faded again, and the computer took over. We went up into Lu space, then the *Revenge* descended again.

As we approached the icy ball of rock, the *Revenge* descended more. Suddenly, the colors stretched, and Lu space vanished in the usual plume of light and heat. The stars reappear.

We'd fallen out short. And the gravity drives were still on.

"What the hell just happened?"

Earl tapped at some screens. "It appears that your instructions to the computer had it descend past the boundary between Lu space and normal space."

The only way out of Lu space was to turn off the gravity field entirely. Even the star sharks did it that way. What had we just discovered?

We'd just done what no one else had ever done. The astonishment welled up in my chest until I had to move. I reached out and slapped Earl's shoulder. "We did it! It works! Yes!"

Earl's voice, accompanied by the barest nod, fell like icy water on my victory. "You have succeeded where all others have failed."

Did the man have any personality at all? Brandy had changed all human space, too. But what I'd done was different from her spectacular flying. I'd used engineering.

Still, when I thought about falling out underneath a blockade, I did not have the required accuracy. Yet.

I let the last of the euphoria drain away and got back to business. "We need more software. I need a model in Virtual Vision so I can see the relationship between Lu space and regular space. What's more is I need the navigation computer to understand that relationship."

"The software would be more your job than mine. What other items will you need?"

I thought about falling out just above the stratosphere and heading down to the planet, landing, and taking off again, with naval ships shooting at me. "A way to hide from gravity scan and radar would be nice."

Earl thought for a moment, tapping on the console. "For gravity scans, you can either turn off your drives or use a decoy. I can tweak your radar countermeasures. In the war, decoy missiles were used a time or two."

I turned the *Revenge* outward again, since I needed to practice more with these weird jumps. An idea began to form in my head, several ideas, plans and contingencies. "Rig me a couple of those decoys, and one bomb that will look like a ship the size of the *Revenge* just blew up. And..."

I thought about flying the planes at Goldblum's Circus back on New Zion. I knew how to use air to turn a plane, or a ship, but not to keep one aloft.

Pursing my lips, I shook my head at how insane this all sounded, how insane I was to take this job. I needed the challenge though, I did. And the money, too.

"I'll also need whatever you can do to make the hull more of a lifting body. Any control surfaces you can add for atmospheric maneuvering wouldn't hurt either."

I hit the jump button. When the stars faded, I wondered how much I could do with the new power coupler installed. A smile grew on my face as I made a slow left turn. The reactor temp stayed right where it was, and the boost light came on. I'd turned in Lu space! Again, something no one had ever done.

Then I tri-modulated the field and descended again, gauging when I would fall out. When I did, with drive still active, I punched it. The drive burst to four-point-seven gs for six seconds.

✦✦✦✦✦

Ten days later, I walked into the Abogada, feeling like the bar, Marta's Place, and Earl's shop were the only places on all of Planeta de Angel that I ever went to. I wondered what the rest of the planet, even the rest of the city, was like.

When I emerged from the dark entry into the light, I walked over and sat at the bar. "Hello, Ramon. How's your family?"

He rolled his eyes as he poured my drink. "Karl wishes us to move to a safe planet, a better place to raise the kids."

I gestured toward two freelancers and three smugglers drinking at the tables. "The man has a point. On the other hand, if someone bothers you or your kids, everyone here will come to your defense."

Ramon set my drink on the bar. "Gracias, Deuce. You are wise. And that man is waiting for you." He pointed toward the lawyer waiting in a booth. "You're taking the suicide mission?"

Smiling, I motioned him closer. "Want to know a secret? I have the best ship in the quadrant. I'll be back."

With a wink, I rose, sauntered over to the booth, and slid in across from my employer, or at least his representative.

"Hello, Ghazi."

He wore a different tailored shirt, but his intense dark eyes still tried to read my mind, to see why I thought I would survive this blockade run. He nodded once. "Deuce. What can I do for you?"

"You should ask what I can do for you. I'm ready. I have an invoice for expenses, itemized. Where is this blockade?"

Ghazi cocked his head. "Why do you think you can do this when everyone else has laughed in my face?"

I pasted the predatory grin of a cocky freelancer on my face. "Because I'm smarter and faster and you bought me a fabulous ship. Plus, your only options are to let me try or give up."

For an answer, Ghazi pulled a data crystal from his pocket and set it next to his computer. "Give me your secure key."

I got out my pad and swiped my public key over to him, along with the invoices for Earl's work, and mine. Ghazi messed with the files for a bit and swiped them to the crystal.

He held it up in two fingers. "This will open for you, but only when you are more than five hundred kilometers from me. It has everything you need. Now, it should take you around ten weeks to get there and back to Earth. We'll give you a ten thousand credit bonus for each day sooner than that."

I could run a few days at a full four gs, compensated back to two, for that kind of money, especially with the new gravinol—medicine to combat the effects of high gravity.

Taking the crystal, I looked at it a moment before putting it in a secure slot on my bracer. An interesting tech to put in such a small crystal. At five hundred kilometers, I would be out in space or at least on a grav-bus to Extranjera.

I rose but turned back to Ghazi. "Get those invoices paid within the hour. That way I know you're good for the money."

I strode out of the bar, giving Ramon half a salute as I did. He looked worried, concerned for my safety. Back in my days at Solomon Tech, alone on the beach during winter break, I'd almost drowned. That day I had fought to live. I would fight to live this time, too.

Out under the dome, with high clouds dancing overhead, I stopped at Marta's Place to get some empanadas to start my trip. Then I walked with a bounce in my step through the tunnel, with its sunshine on the peak. On the way, I ordered more food for the journey. I hadn't planned on ten weeks, and half with a passenger, too.

An old man hobbled up next to me. I turned, expecting someone asking for money, and found retired Admiral Jackson.

He winked at me. "I knew you'd be in on this, Burgundy."

He'd been my sister Brandy's commander and friend, and he'd trained me at the academy when the bastards who made me had forced me to go there. I barely recognized him without a uniform. If he could find me, others could, too.

I scowled. "What? What are you doing here?"

He held up a hand. "Relax. Remember, I'm one of the few people who knows what ship you're flying. Besides, I'm retired and exploring the galaxy. No one cares."

I ground my teeth together. "Are they still watching me?"

Jackson snorted. "As near as I can tell, they're still wondering how you vanished so thoroughly. Cinti did some financial gymnastics so the purchase of that ship couldn't be traced back to her." He paused a moment and looked me in the eye. "Rumor has it you took the suicide mission."

I rolled my eyes. "I'm coming back."

Jackson smiled. "Well, you will be facing half a Roman fleet. Still, don't forget to ask why this place is so important."

I shoved Jackson. "I'm just a chauffeur, old man. Bigger heads than me will know what's important."

He stopped as we reached the end of the tunnel where it opened into the spaceport. "Sure, but what fun would that be?"

I turned to walk backwards a few steps. He did have a point, though was he expecting me to be like Brandy? He never had before. Uncertain what he expected or if I cared, I headed on back to Earl's.

★★★★★

Two hours later, Ghazi had sent the money, and I'd paid Earl three hundred thousand. My extra food had come in and been stowed on board. Earl and I, along with Roberre, stood at the bottom of the *Revenge's* ramp with little more to say.

I wanted to pull him down and kiss him, if just on the cheek. Instead, I cuffed his rock-hard shoulder. "Thank you for all your work."

Earl offered his hand. "You are welcome. Let me know how it goes."

As I shook his hand, Roberre rubbed up against my leg. I bent down to pet his metal head. So strange. "I will be in touch."

"Wuff," Roberre said.

With a sigh, wishing they could come along to keep me company, I gave a little wave. "Goodbye, both of you."

I climbed up the ramp, starting it closing as I did, and then up the ladder to the personnel deck. I strode to the cockpit, sat, jacked in, and powered up. As the vibrations spread through my body, I changed my mind. Here, in *Hiram's Revenge*, I wanted to be alone. Safe and alone.

Moments later, I flew the *Revenge* to the other side of Earl's now open shop and out the bottom over the Precipice. Pointing the nose upward, I climbed through the atmosphere. I let the air take me where it would, testing the new control surfaces. Turn into the wind. Catch a thermal. I still used the gravity drive to climb, though.

Coming down again, on the other end of this trip, was going to be interesting.

Soon, I left the plumes of acrid smoke and swirling heat behind. The sky faded to black, and the stars appeared. A few minutes later, I backed the drives off to zero, though I was still headed outward.

I retrieved the crystal from my bracer and put it into the slot beside the pilot's seat. Information popped up in my Virtual Vision. First, the navigation data showed I had to go north of the Angel's Planet ecliptic fifty-eight light years. From there it was only thirty-four to Earth.

The star system itself made me gasp. It was an orange star. That would make the habitable zone much closer to the star than most places. Even then, it wouldn't be warm. And I was supposed to use a specifically coded tight-beam laser transmission to an array on the planet. The passenger could get to any place on the planet within one day.

I was then to take this unnamed person to a ranch in the Rocky Mountains west of Denver on Earth. That was it.

Well, that was it except for the two battleships, two carriers, a hundred or more fighters, and twenty-five destroyers. Speed and stealth were the only way.

I adjusted my course and accelerated to Lu space, where no one could find me, and I could live with no expectations. For a while.

4
ORANGE STAR

I floated in the outskirts of my destination orange star system, a K3 sun. Arriving at a place like this, seeing the sights in my telescope, in my glorious solitude being where so few humans had ever been, was what I'd glimpsed in my first simulator flight on the *Carpathia* headed for Solomon Tech.

Picking up a passenger was the last thing I wanted to do, except I needed the money.

An orange star was such a strange place to settle a colony. With the orbital information in Ghazi's crystal, my navigation system had found all the planets in only about eight hours. The inhabited one currently sat on the far side of the star, a little to the right.

The question was whether the Romans had enough ships to put pickets floating dark and silent at any likely hiding or entry places. Regardless, I had to get closer to send that message and maybe locate a landing site. Based on Brandy's biography, during the war the Romans had put pickets everywhere in their home system. Then again, this wasn't their home system. They wouldn't have as many ships.

I could sit here for days trying to find the perfect site for my next jump. There was a gas giant even farther to the right of the star. It had several moons, one of which I could scoot in behind, so a double hiding place. My momentum would carry me past both the moon and the gas giant. Then I could get a clear view of the planet.

Before I could come up with a reason not to, I accelerated toward that moon. I flat-shifted, moving main thrust around behind me, so *Hiram's Revenge* flew nose-forward rather than top forward. That was bad for walking around, but good for maneuvering. My navigation computer calculated where the moon would be when I got there, and I set a jump where it would tri-modulate the field and dump me out as gently as can be, but with drives off this time. It also gave me a practice run at getting close to a planet.

Just as my misgivings grew, I hit the jump button. Twenty seconds later, the *Revenge* started down again. Eighteen seconds after that, the graph said I was just above real space. The drive cut out and the *Revenge* fell. My body drifted up, held in place by the straps, as my own weight lifted off me. The colors stretched and brightened into a light plume. The stars appeared as the light and heat dispersed.

I zipped over the moon, its icy crags just four hundred kilometers to my right. I would need to get closer to the planet for the pickup run.

A blip appeared in my Virtual Vision; a ship firing up its gravity drive. It was five hundred thousand kilometers away, near a different moon. I was seconds behind reality. I could not catch it. Even if I could, I couldn't fight a warship. The blockade would know I was here.

Dozens more light plumes appeared. The blockade ships had found me!

I had to get out of here. My finger reached to start my drives.

But why would they send that many ships after me? They would have to have abandoned the entire blockade. I quelled my panic. Wait. Be patient.

Five of the new blips vanished again. They reappeared in plumes in front of the fleeing ship.

"Record!"

Explosions lit the night. Ships flew left and right. The fight did not last long. Soon, four light plumes expanded from ships returning to join the fleet.

I just breathed, hoping they hadn't seen my dark ship.

"Stop recording. Replay. Enhance and magnify."

The ship had recorded where my eyes pointed, so what I saw first was the battle. Due to the time to enhance the image, it played in slow motion. A destroyer accelerated away from me. I didn't see any markings. I assumed it was a Roman ship.

Then the five light plumes appeared, disgorging star sharks.

The destroyer, which had been on high alert, possibly thinking me another destroyer, had fired immediately. The sharks had as well, as they came out of Lu space. Thirty missiles arced toward the destroyer. Five went from destroyer to sharks. The destroyer's lasers took out twenty missiles. The other ten turned the destroyer to a ball of flame and shrapnel. The sharks dodged, but one was not fast enough.

Based on what I was seeing, the others had taken damage, too.

On the recording, my gaze had turned toward the large fleet of ships when the remaining sharks had come back. Fifty or a hundred sharks headed for another of the gas giant's moons, behind me. As far as I knew, no one had ever seen even a dozen sharks together at the same place.

Either the sharks hadn't noticed me, or a dark, unpowered object flying by was not something they cared about. That meant accelerating away was out of the question.

My navigation computer showed I was in a hyperbolic orbit around the gas giant. Eventually that should take me out of sight of the sharks, or at least far enough away they couldn't catch me. I did have a boost charge. That would help, though I wanted some for the getaway.

For a time, I just watched the star sharks with my passive sensor arrays, mostly quantum telescopes. Some things that none of the literature mentioned became apparent. First, there were different sizes. The smallest seemed to be shepherded by the bigger ones. Those couldn't be children, could they? Moreover, all of them cavorted, bumping each other, and even dancing. Some of the bigger ones dove to the outer reaches of the gas giant, but they didn't stay long. They even seemed to hesitate before rushing down, and at the bottom they appeared to flatten out somewhat.

I could have watched them for hours, but my stomach growled, and my bladder demanded attention. Being in freefall made some routine tasks more difficult, or more fun. I jacked out, unbuckled, and propelled myself down the corridor to the head. On the way back, I grabbed food from the galley—my own empanadas. While nowhere near as good as Marta's, they were easy to eat in zero-g. I made my way back to the bridge, ate, and slept while my telescopes and gravity scans gathered more information about the sharks and my destination planet.

I drifted closer to that strange, inhabited planet.

Soon, I would need to make contact.

I dreamed of star sharks gathering around me, nuzzling and sniffing. I wanted to get away but couldn't. Even more came, close, strange, curious, and dangerous.

✶✶✶✶✶

When I woke, still in the pilot's seat on *Hiram's Revenge*, I shuddered at the dream. To clear my head and let the memory fade, I got to work. I'd cleared the gas giant enough to make laser contact. The planet was only twenty light-minutes away now, so I set my navigation computer to mapping the gravity drive traffic around the odd planet. And I worked to locate the antenna I would send the message to. The crystal had longitude and latitude, plus a landmark to measure from.

From this distance I couldn't see details on the planet, even with my best magnification. I could find the continents and oceans, which gave me a clue how strange this planet was. How did people live there? First, like in the model I'd seen, it had an icecap not at the pole, but at the equator on the night side. That meant it was tidally locked. My angle was bad, but it looked like there might be an ocean opposite, on the sunward side. Clouds obscured the twilight areas most of the way around. There was one other ocean I could see, near the twilight.

I had my computer overlay the map I'd gotten on Ghazi's crystal with my telescope view. A mountain range showed up on one side of that ocean near the twilight, with what appeared to be their main city on the other shore. The rivers all seemed to flow out from the twilight, and all the human habitations extended north and south from that main city, with nothing more than a thousand kilometers from the twilight area.

Why would anyone choose to settle this world? Then again, Angel had chosen hell itself for his planet, but he'd done that specifically to keep ordinary people away.

Ghazi's overlay let me pinpoint the coordinates I needed. Then I had to wait three more hours for the *Revenge* to be at an angle where I could hit the receiver antenna with my laser communication array.

At last, the time came, and I recorded the message. "This is Captain Deuce. I am here to take an emissary to Earth. I need an isolated place to land tomorrow, just into the night side. I will come in from light to dark. You will see my descent through the atmosphere. Be ready and be fast."

Then I waited. Forty minutes round trip time, plus some time to find a location. In the meantime, I plotted courses of the blockade ships, looking for patterns.

Almost I wished I could go back and film the star sharks. They had come here for some specific reason. What was it?

At last, my answer came from the planet. "We acknowledge your presence and are grateful. Our freedom depends on your success because we have no military. Please land at Taimana Gletscher in the dark in nineteen timer. We are sending koordinater and a terrain map."

Data came through into my buffers. I had to run it through the conversion algorithms on Ghazi's crystal before I could bring them up in my Virtual Vision. When I did, their map showed a location perhaps ten kilometers into the dark side a few hundred kilometers from the main city where that mountain range extended back into the darkness. Zooming in let me see jagged peaks rising above a trapezoidal glacier that angled down into a valley to the north.

I sent back an acknowledgement, hoping "timer" meant hours, then spent the next two hours running through courses and options, honing everything to the finest detail. The biggest thing was I needed to come in from sunward, the opposite side of the planet from where I was now.

At last, feeling like I was overthinking everything, I got out of the pilot's seat and pushed off. I floated down the corridor to the common room. There I did some zero-g gymnastics like I'd done in high school. After that, I ate some more and went to sleep in my own bed, strapped in for the night.

When the alarm woke me, I reversed the process; food in the galley first, then working out in zero-g in the common room, and finally floating back along the corridor to the cockpit. There, I strapped into the recessed pilot's seat, jacked in, and ran my course through the navigation computer again. When going up against a fleet of warships, a little obsession might make all the difference.

The time came. I lit up the *Revenge's* gravity drives and accelerated sunward, wondering how my sister would break this blockade.

I patted the seat next to me. "Well, Hiram, it's time you earned your pay."

I hit the jump button.

5
GOING DOWN

The *Revenge* dropped out of Lu space, drives still active and still in empty space, seven light minutes out. This time I had the right angle to approach the planet. The light plume would be clearly visible to the blockade fleet. They would come investigate. With the time lag, I would be gone.

I punched the *Revenge* back toward the planet with a full boost.

With the course pre-planned, I hit the jump button again. As soon as the stars faded, the computer backed off to a sedate two gs. Then it began to descend.

The planet grew large on my gravity scan. Really large. I was about to hit the fallout button when the *Revenge* slid out of Lu space fifty kilometers above the stratosphere. The light plume would be visible, but above the daytime planet, the blockade ships might not notice.

I pushed the nose down and accelerated. The air buffeted the *Revenge* as I entered the atmosphere.

Above me, the blockade ships would assume I was decelerating, messing with their targeting.

I jigged left. Then I extended the airfoils Earl had added. Flames from reentry enveloped *Hiram's Revenge*. Smoke trailed behind.

Below, I could see the twilight, an angled, rising line of darkness.

"Arm decoy one."

The *Revenge* beeped at me. I jigged left again.

I hit full deceleration. The altitude counted down in my Virtual Vision. The flames around the hull dissipated. The smoke trail faded.

Hiram and I reached six thousand meters. Twilight came.

"Fire decoy."

The missile launched. I shut down the gravity drive and lifted the *Revenge's* nose into the wind. We headed east into darkness.

Below, the missile slammed into a mountain. The explosion sent a shockwave through the air. The flash would be clearly visible from orbit. Now, if they only believed it.

The air buffeted the *Revenge*. The ship didn't really glide, more like a controlled fall. Flare out. Keep the nose up. Ride the wind down.

In the dark, the last ridge loomed. My Virtual Vision gave me an alarm. I was coming in too low. I pulled the nose up even more. I tipped the *Revenge* right to avoid the highest point. We cleared the rock by five meters.

A thermal caught me. Then I was too high. I tipped the nose down. The glacier loomed below.

"Deploy landing skids. Open rear airlock."

I tipped the nose up. Down we came. The *Revenge* bounced off the ice. It went back up, then down again. It bounced a second time. We landed and skidded across the ice. I fought to keep my ship straight. And to stop.

The front skid collapsed. The nose dug up a shower of ice and snow. The *Revenge* came to a halt twenty meters from the end of the ice and a rock wall.

"Retract skids."

I didn't need them to take off. I would be going straight up.

A figure dashed out onto the ice in front of me. Cold air from the open door reached the bridge. The person must have seen the light and ran for the rear.

I flipped on the intercom and the internal cameras.

When the person reached the top of the ladder, she pushed her hood back and hesitated. She had a bag over each shoulder.

"Get in here. Drop the bags in the first room on the right. Then straight forward and strap in."

I shut off the intercom and closed the rear airlock.

Now I just had to get back to space. My hands itched to get moving. The longer we took, the more likely the blockade ships would find us. Without waiting, I powered up the drives and lifted us off the ground.

I slid the *Revenge* backward and right.

My passenger came sliding into the bridge.

I pushed us straight up. Gravity pressed me into my seat. A plasma cannon blast hit the glacier. The shockwave tossed us farther away. My passenger levered herself into the seat.

Tilting the nose up, I put thrust behind us.

"Strap in. Plug in the helmet. Put it on."

Six missiles descended through the atmosphere. I turned away from them and pushed farther south, still climbing. The missiles curved toward me, tracking on radar.

"Oh!" my passenger said. She must have found the Virtual Vision.

I flipped laser cannon fire control to her seat. "Trigger on the right joystick. Whatever you look at, the cannon will hit. Anything up here is an enemy."

She looked upward and pulled the trigger. Laser fire erupted in my Virtual Vision. The closest missile exploded, fireworks in the night sky.

My passenger said, "Got it."

I dodged left and right, still tending up. Twice more my passenger fired the laser cannon. Two more missiles became fireworks. Kilometers above, the blockade launched another nine. A squadron of fighters flew down into the atmosphere. The twelve fighters split into three groups, trying to box me in

My mouth went dry. "That doesn't look good."

I'd never been in real combat. And all the simulations had ships with more than one lousy laser turret. And never twelve against one either.

My goal was not to fight. It was to escape. And I wanted to hide the *Revenge's* capabilities as much as possible.

Off to my left, in the twilight, lightning strobed. A storm? I shifted our angle of ascent away from the fighters and toward the lightning. A dark patch with no stars visible behind meant a thunderhead.

My passenger blew up another missile and hit a fighter, but it was still too far to hurt it much. The little ship stayed after us. The fighter fired its own lasers. It hit our turret.

More fighters descended ahead of me. I needed to reach the cloud cover.

My passenger turned toward a missile and pulled the trigger. Nothing happened. She tried four times.

A missile closed in from behind. I jigged left. I dropped my nose. The air pushed me down. The missile got closer and exploded. Shrapnel ripped into the *Revenge*.

I swore. No red lights came on, though. The bulkhead doors all slammed shut, sealing us on the bridge.

Wind buffeted the *Revenge*. I went with the currents, figuring these pilots had never flown in a storm. Wisps of cloud swirled around us. I banked left. A thermal drove us up.

We neared the thunderhead, about halfway up its height. Radar showed four fighters coming into the clouds from the other side. The ones behind and above were closing in. This would be close.

"Arm decoy two."

The *Revenge* beeped.

As soon as the dark clouds swirled in around us, I lifted the nose. Then punched the gravity drive. We went straight up. Three fighters launched missiles.

"Fire. Boost. Jump."

6
IN-FLIGHT REPAIRS

As the thunderstorm's internal winds tossed the *Revenge*, the decoy launched. The gravity drives hit five gs, pushing us back in our seats. The jump light went on. The dark clouds stretched and faded. The amorphous colors outside seemed obscured by something.

I immediately backed off to three gs. The boost light came on again.

I checked our course. We weren't even close to heading toward Earth. I could have done the standard maneuver of falling out and changing course before jumping again. But why would I want to do that?

My passenger squirmed in her seat. "What happened? Where are we?"

I didn't answer until my navigation computer found the course to Earth using only gravity scan. When the green line appeared, I did a combination vertical shift and course change. We ended up headed toward Earth, top first so gravity would be down toward the deck. Last, I enabled the gravity compensators, reducing our three g acceleration to an effective one here inside.

I relaxed until I remembered I had a damaged ship. My stomach bent in knots. They'd hurt *Hiram's Revenge!*

Taking some long, slow breaths, I answered my passenger. "That was a jump to Lu space. As far as I know, it has never been done from an atmosphere before."

I cycled through my readouts. The reactor and gravity drives seemed fine. The front skid had a warning, which I knew about. The laser turret showed offline. There was a hull breach in the cargo bay and another in the common room out back. But the air pressure out there only showed a little low, not vacuum.

My passenger gestured toward the outside. "And what is Lu space?"

"Um…" She'd distracted me, but she didn't know what Lu space was? The only way that was possible would be a colony isolated for at least fifty years. "Well, it's a gravity anomaly that lets us get to Earth in about a month."

She didn't answer for what seemed an eternity. "A month. Huh. That explains a lot."

I jacked out and removed my helmet. "We have a lot to talk about, but first there are repairs we need to do. When I looked over, I noticed she not only had her helmet on, but she was wearing a heavy coat, too. That couldn't be comfortable. "Oh, you can unbuckle and take the helmet off now. The coat, too."

"Oh." She gestured at the helmet. "So we don't have to stay…"

"For a month? No. We have actual beds and everything." Then I remembered; Brandy had done exactly that. She'd flown in a single-seat fighter non-stop for twenty-nine days.

I helped my passenger jack out and get standing up. She had straw colored hair and appeared maybe fortyish. Something about her reminded me of Admiral Cinte Arias's wife Joyce, though they looked nothing alike. Perhaps she had Joyce's unconscious beauty and grace.

She shed her coat as took in her surroundings. "What is galt with the ship? Are we in danger? Is it usually wet out there?"

Following her gaze, what the sensors had been saying suddenly made sense. "Oh. No. We jumped to Lu space from inside a thunderstorm. We brought some of it with us."

What had that done to the storm? A chunk of atmosphere had just vanished. It would have been a hell of a thunderclap.

She laid a hand on my arm. "Excuse me, I am out of my faktor, so I must apologize. Let me introduce myself. I am Ambassador Mikka Retts."

This woman had no stake in my life, no connection to the bastards who created me, meaning I could talk to her. On the other hand, she was an ambassador to the Council of Planets on Earth. The bastards would be there, and she would be talking to them.

"I am called Deuce."

Ambassador Retts blinked a moment. "That is not your ry, um, name, then. It is a...what is the word?"

Stepping over to the bulkhead door, I checked the display there. It showed air on the other side, but at a rather lower pressure.

I glanced over my shoulder at Ambassador Retts. "Alias. And yes, there are people who would hurt me if they knew my identity."

She pressed her lips together then looked me in the eye. "It seems I have much to learn. On our trip to Earth, will you teach me?"

If I was right about this planet being isolated for fifty or more years, she would need to know a lot. I laid a hand on the door. "I will do what I can. First, let us reclaim the rest of my ship."

I brought up the ship controls on my bracer. "This door isn't opening until we reduce the pressure in here."

Once I typed the commands, the *Revenge* sucked some of the air out of the bridge. It got colder and harder to breathe. "Let's be quick."

I cranked the lever and opened the bulkhead door. Cold air blasted into the bridge. Condensation lined the walls in the corridor. This was going to be a mess.

Walking to the common room at the rear winded me. I felt a headache starting.

In the top left corner, two holes gaped through the inner and outer hull, leaving the inside jagged. One piece of shrapnel lay on the deck, covered in dew that looked ready to freeze. The other had made a hole in the floor.

"We need to..."

Ambassador Retts finished my sentence, panting. "Get oxygen."

"Right. Back to the bridge."

We went back. I got out the light EVA suits from a cabinet built into the wall beside the door. I pulled it over my flight suit, and the fabric sealed me in of its own accord, the opening in the chest closed together as if by magic. The gloves tightened around my fingers. The oxygen tank on the back weighed me down. Then I retrieved our helmets, putting my own on first. The suit sealed itself to the helmet, too. Air started flowing.

While Ambassador Retts started pulling her suit on, a bit puzzled by the lack of button or zipper, I stood and breathed. My head cleared and I began to get the tasks in order.

Once I'd helped Ambassador Retts finish sealing her suit, she put her helmet back on. I flicked on the internal comms. "First, we clean the edges of those holes a bit, then we build the matrix and apply the hull sealant."

I led the ambassador out through the short corridor to the common room and down the ladder to the cargo deck. The repair kit was in a cabinet at the engineering station directly across from the ladder. The kit had its own little computer with it, and a transmitter. I'd never used the kit, though I had gone over the instructions. I opted for the hole by the ladder down here first.

I found the molecular grinder in a drawer and handed it to the ambassador. "Please clean up the edges. It doesn't need to be perfect. Some raggedness will help the matrix bind to the hull."

The ambassador looked at the device and went over to the hole. Puzzled, she flipped the switch and applied the grinder to a jagged edge sticking out into the cargo hold. It buzzed and dust fell on the floor.

She stopped and looked at the device. "Huh."

As she started back in, I pulled out the wand with the mesh already wrapped around it. "That's good enough. Go on up and do the two up there."

After plugging the wand into the computer, I stuck it into the hole. The ambassador paused on the ladder to see what I was doing. I turned the wand, and a 3D image of the hole appeared on the little screen. I used my finger to draw on the screen where I wanted the matrix to go, inside and outside of both the inner and outer hull.

Again, I turned the wand. The wire mesh matrix expanded to fill the hole. At the four spots I'd selected, it expanded more, mushrooming so it would form barriers inside and out. When it looked good, I hit the next button on the computer. This time, the wand turned on its own, spraying sealant. When it hit the matrix, it sizzled and expanded. As the wand turned, it pulled out, spraying more sealant. It reminded me a little of a 3D printer, but with an extra catalyst phase.

When the wand reached the edge, it flashed. The ceramic-steel alloy hardened and sealed itself to the hull. But it didn't match my sleek black ship. My refuge had been damaged, broken. A shudder grew in my chest. I wanted to go hide in my quarters and not come out, maybe ever. Or I wanted to blow up every ship in that blockade. *Hiram's Revenge* had been damaged. It would never be the same.

I touched the stupid-looking mushroom sticking out of the wall and gave myself time to think. I took long slow breaths. Reason returned, and my fury grew cold and calculating. They would pay, of that I would make sure. Since a direct assault would be suicide, that left Jackson's question: what did the Romans want? They didn't want the ambassador to get to Earth, for one. Getting her there would be a good start.

With a sigh, I headed up the ladder to fix the other holes, which took maybe five minutes.

The ambassador examined the wand when I finished. At last, she handed it back to me, and I packed it away.

She gestured at the dripping walls. "Forbavsendeg! What's next? The water?"

I looked around, pressing my lips together. "Well, we need to test those plugs, which will be difficult with the air outside. We clean up the bedrooms, and the furniture out here. Then we suck the air outside in here."

An hour later, we headed back to the bridge. We'd vacuumed out the couches in the common room and folded them into the floor. Then we'd cleaned up the bedrooms, put

linens and most of my clothes into the sonic cleaner and
sealed those doors.

I grabbed the last of my empanadas on the way past the
galley. When we closed the bulkhead door, sealing us on the
bridge, I used my bracer to bring the air pressure back up to
normal in the small room with rain on the canopy.

We took off the helmets, stripped out of the pressure
suits, and sat down in the recessed chairs, ignoring the
joysticks. I reset the environmental controls to evacuate all
the air from the rest of the ship. That would take most of the
water out, too. The recyclers would catch the water, and the
bedrooms, though sealed, were still connected to the air
supply, so those would be in vacuum, too.

While we waited, I put the empanadas in the food box by
my seat and had it heat them up. When they were ready, I
handed two to the ambassador.

"What are these? Some kind of meat tærte?" She bit into
one.

I hid my smile by taking a bite, savoring the spicy
sausage and sauce. "Some kind, yes."

"Oh!" Ambassador Retts put a hand over her mouth. "Oh,
dear."

Chuckling, I handed her a water bottle. "And these are
mild compared to Marta's back home."

Was Angel's Planet home? No, *Hiram's Revenge* was
home, but I had no other planet to call home. I stopped with
an empanada halfway to my mouth. That one biography said
Brandy had never had a home either, but for a different
reason: her fame meant she was recognizable anywhere. I
existed because of her fame. Getting away from the bastards
who created me had left me with no home either. I'd done
what I had to do I could get away, but what did I want for
myself?

The Ambassador held up a second empanada. "I knew
det, when I came, that I would have new, um, experiences, on
this trip. I wasn't expecting them so soon." She took a timid
bite.

The air system beeped, telling me we'd reached near-
vacuum.

I waved a water bottle at the door behind us. "Time for part two."

I went through the sequence for an emergency override on the rear airlock door. It took about six approvals and a security code, with good reason. At last, the alarm sounded and both airlock doors opened. With the *Revenge* still set to vacuum, the water on the canopy ran up and back as the air got pulled inside.

I chuckled at a perverse thought, perhaps coming from a professor at Solomon Tech. "We could calculate how long this is going to take. The Lu space bubble is about half a meter outside the ship, but it's an ovoid not a sphere. And then we subtract the volume of the ship."

Ambassador Retts looked over and raised an eyebrow. "That seems...vel, unnecessary."

"Quite. I'm just an engineer. Waiting generates strange thoughts."

My air tanks would be full for sure.

The ambassador yawned just as the *Revenge* beeped that we had reached vacuum again. I closed the rear airlock again and started filling the ship with air.

"Ambassador Retts, you can sleep there if you want. Or your quarters will be ready in another minute or two."

She clambered out of the co-pilot's seat and looked down at me. "I assume that the beds are more komfortabel? And call me Mikka." She yawned again.

I got up to join her, my muscles weary, adrenalin draining from my body. I yawned myself. "Let's get some sleep. Tomorrow we'll talk."

Twenty minutes later, I had Mikka bedded down on freshly laundered sheets and stepped into my own quarters. I'd already been to the head, so I stripped out of my flight suit and laid down on the bed, more of a cot attached to the wall. Still, it had the same smart foam that the pilot's seat had. The mattress conformed to my body, making a comfortable nest.

I closed my eyes, but sleep eluded me. The front skid had collapsed on that glacier. We hadn't fixed that yet. It wouldn't affect the flight, just the landing, and it was in the outer hull, open to vacuum. That skid would be difficult to repair. Plus, I had just pulled off a rescue that Brandy might have done. It felt good.

One thought bothered me more than all the rest. A hundred star sharks and a Roman blockade surrounded Mikka's planet. But why?

7
MIKKA

The next morning, when Mikka woke, I was in the galley trying to make waffles. Fortunately, the auto-stove could make up for most of my failings. I had two waffles, or two-thirds of two waffles with crusty, partial edges. The fried vat-grown ham was only partly burned.

Mikka when she saw, or maybe smelled breakfast, chuckled. "Let me hjælp. I can probably do worse."

Together we butchered breakfast and carried it, along with coffee, out to the common room where I'd pulled the table from the floor earlier. We sat across from each other on plastic chairs also extruded from the floor.

Mikka poured syrup on her waffles then looked up at me and sniffed at the coffee. "Is this some kind of tea?"

"Not exactly."

She took a drink and choked. "Gah! What is that?"

"Um...coffee." I took my own drink while thinking it through. She lived on a cold planet, where coffee would not grow. "An acquired taste."

"I'll say." She took another sip and shuddered. "You don't have tea?"

The irony made me laugh. "Well, I never appreciated it much."

Mikka gave me a withering look, then shook her head and tried one more time on the coffee, with the same result. She regarded me with hooded eyes. "Tell me all."

I opened my mouth and found nothing to say. "I know less than you, right now. Tell me about your planet, and what happened with the Roman blockade. For that matter, what do you call your planet?"

She took a bite of ham and spoke clearly around the mouthful. "It's called Eksil. The blockade surprised us. About two years ago, a ship found us and traded a few things. We thought we would soon be back in touch with Earth. Then last year, the Romans showed up and told us we were part of the Nova Roman Empire, one of their colony planets. We objected, but they rather ignoreret us."

That first ship must have found something.

I rubbed my chin. "Were the star sharks there when the first trade ship came?"

"Star sharks? What are those?"

"Aliens. I saw them out by that nearest gas giant."

Mikka perked up, fork halfway to her mouth. "Oh! I hadn't hørt they were back. No. They come back every three or four years. When the astronomers first found them a century ago, no one believed them."

A century? I snorted juice through my nose. After I finished coughing and blowing my nose, I looked up in astonishment. "A century? How long have people been on this planet?"

"Um, just over two hundred years. We were settled by the *Sydney-Copenhagen*."

I dropped my fork. It clattered from the table onto the floor.

After Thurman Pauley had founded the Tau Ceti colony and returned to Earth, the world governments had launched eight juggernaut class colony ships. Two had gone to Thurman, the remaining six to other promising planets. Five of those had arrived and had created the colonies that were now full members of the Council of Planets. The sixth, the *Sydney-Copenhagen,* had been presumed lost.

Bending to retrieve my fork, I found Mikka staring. I gestured at her, open-handed. "The crew of that ship must have performed super-human heroics to find any planet at all."

Mikka gave me a slight nod. "That is the way we mindes them. Do our origins explain the Roman actions?"

I had to consider that, so I took another bite of waffle. "Not entirely, I think. Being settled sub-light may give you privileges and may shake up the Council Planets, but I don't see how the Romans would gain much from that. Besides, the blockade suggests they want to *stop* you from disrupting the Council of Planets. How did you contact me anyway?"

Mikka turned one hand up while stabbing the waffle with the other. "That puzzled us, too. When the Romans arrived, they etableret a government office on the planet. One day, we got an anonymous message that told us to select someone to go to Earth as ambassador and to point one of our antennas spaceward to wait for your signal."

That part made sense, so I nodded. "The Council of Planets must have a spy, most likely several, in the Roman military."

Scowling, Mikka shook her head. "This idea of militaries and spies is so fremmed to us. Why don't people just talk and get along? Work for the fælles good?"

I had to struggle not to laugh, not to drop my fork again. I ended up just doing a statue imitation.

The woman had a point. How would Thurman have reacted if they'd been the last colony found by jump ships? That Thurman had decided to share jump technology rather than use it to rule all human space was a testament to just what Mikka was saying. Then again, none of the colonies could really stand up to Earth long term. There were just too many people there.

She made me think back to my political science classes at Solomon Tech. Whoever hired me should have sent a teacher along on this trip. I sipped coffee to see if the bitterness generated any other thoughts. It didn't. "I'm not sure I'm the best person to answer these questions."

Mikka smiled and patted my hand. "For the next month, you are what I have, and I need to know a lot more before I get to Earth."

True. If she didn't understand Earth politics before she got there, they would eat her alive.

I took another bite of now-cold waffle and thought. "Well, I think it's about self-interest. If an individual or a group thinks standing in opposition is best for them, they will. And at times, they see gaining power as what is best for them."

"Power?" Mikka knit her brow, puzzled. "But people who think that way wouldn't be qualified for such jobs. How do they get the positions?"

She'd flabbergasted me again. Perhaps I was just too cynical. "Um...popularity or knowing someone else in power. There are many ways."

Mikka took a breath and drained her juice, slowly. "In other words, the people I negotiate with on Earth will have neither Eksil's nor mankind's best interests in mind."

A smile grew on my face. "You're getting the idea. Most won't, though some will, and others think their interests *are* mankind's best interest. And some will give you what you want to get what they want."

Mikka pointed at the back of the ship, which was the wrong direction. "And that brings us back to what the Romans want."

By then we'd both finished eating, so I got up and collected dishes from the little table. Together we trooped back down the hall to the galley and loaded everything in the tiny sonic cleaner, food and all.

Once I'd started it, Mikka looked around at the tiny galley. "Where does the food waste go?"

"With the rest of the waste; into a tank that we recycle at our next port. Bigger ships would make mulch out of it and feed it to the plants or even the meat growing vats."

I headed back to the common room, where I used my bracer to fold the table and chairs into the floor and extrude a couch from the side wall opposite the ladder. I settled into it and gestured for Mikka to join me.

Mikka sat next to me, leaving a little space. "What *do* the Romans want?"

I rubbed my chin. "I guess some history is in order. Around sixty years ago my...a pilot and a physicist first fought three of those star sharks that you see so often." I waved at what was outside. "In that process, they discovered Lu space." I indicated our surroundings. "And everything changed. There was a war with Nova Roma, who didn't want to join the Council of Planets. Interestingly, the star sharks joined the war, making it a three-way fight. It ended with the Romans joining the council."

Mikka scowled. "Those star sharks, as you call them, have never bothered us."

She kept surprising me, though maybe that wasn't a surprise. "It's possible they didn't know you were there, but they have also never gone that close to a star. They tend to stay among the outer planets."

First, Mikka looked worried, then hopeful. "Maybe they'll chase off the Romans." Then she shook her head. "We can't formode we'll be so lucky. What came next?"

I hadn't thought about the sharks chasing off the Romans. A hundred of them certainly could. "What happened next was a diaspora. We built ships and headed to the stars. The important part for you, though, is that the Council of Planets consists of those colonies that were settled by sub-light ships. The dozens of frontier planets are all officially colonies of one or another of the council planets."

Mikka raised a hand. "What? Wait. The Romans want to make us their colony, meaning they would control us? So that we have no rights before the council?"

I put my arm up and tapped the back of the couch. "That is what they are doing. Why they would take such a big risk—that blockade is a huge risk—is not clear. Now, the people who sent the spy that got me here have their own motives. At a guess, they want to get you full council membership, but that has other implications. The bigger frontier planets are pushing for their own membership, and no planets have been added to the council since the peace treaty was signed after the war ended. Someone may be angling to use Eksil as a lever to get that done."

Mikka rose and paced, hands behind her back. "Which would leave me caught between the two factions."

I leaned forward on the couch, putting my elbows on my knees. "That does about cover it."

She whirled on me, hands on hips. "There's one more thing. How fast is your ship?"

Why did she need to know that? "Fast, but there are faster ones."

Mikka flopped back onto the couch, frowning. "Can the Romans beat us to Earth?"

Oh. Hell. "Yes, I'm afraid they can."

8
SOL SYSTEM

Almost a month later, Mikka's voice crackled over the intercom, even as she slurred the words. "Deuce, why don't you use your real name?"

Pressed uncomfortably down into the *Revenge's* pilot's seat by too much gravity, I growled. "Because no one can know who I am."

I sounded petulant and angry to my own ears, so I backed off the acceleration, bringing the *Revenge* down to standard thrust that could be compensated to one g.

I immediately breathed easier. The gravinol had worn off sooner this time. We'd been pushing the speed both to surprise the Romans and to maybe get that bonus, too. This was our third time, and we hadn't made forty hours. Fortunately, the gravinol let us sleep through most of it.

The green line still stretched out ahead, toward Earth. The graph in my Virtual Vision showed us climbing higher and higher away from normal space, as expected. This jump, with so many ships and satellites around Earth, I needed to fall out like a regular ship. No special abilities.

We were only a day away now, and I still had to repair the front landing strut.

I flicked on the intercom. "How about we cook something hot to eat?"

"Show me how to make empanadas," Mikka said.

The woman had an adventurous streak, that was sure. She liked to learn new things. Plus, as with going into Eksil, having food ready going into Earth would be a good idea. It would give us flexibility.

I jacked out of Virtual Vision and took my helmet off. "They take a while. We'll snack between."

With great care, I climbed out of the pilot's seat, stopping to sit on the edge. I stretched out my back, shoulders, and legs. It took ten minutes before I got to my feet, making sure all the effects of the time at two gs were worked out.

At last, we both made it to the galley. I started a cup of coffee and brought up the empanada recipe on the galley computer. I hit the start button and the system dumped flour and the rest of the ingredients for the batter into the mixer. Then it heated the oven and the stove. When I set the frying pan on the stove, the system dropped in sausage, onion, chili powder and other spices.

Mikka looked at me with hooded eyes, then gestured to the stove. "You call that cooking? Your computer is doing all the værk!"

I laughed. "Most people cook this way now. We still have to do *some* work." I stirred the sausage to illustrate the point.

Chuckling, Mikka grabbed the cup of coffee and poured half a cup of sugar and creamer into it. She did start another cup for me, though.

That gave me an idea. If I remembered correctly, I had some biscotti somewhere in the freezer. I brought up the inventory and found them.

By the time the system had them thawed, the mixer was rolling out nice, round portions of dough, like little uncooked pizzas. I handed one biscotti to Mikka and dunked the other in my coffee. I took a bite before spooning sausage onto the first bit of dough. Then I folded the circle over and crimped it with a fork.

Dunking her biscotti too, she took a bite before browsing through the filling ingredients on the computer, Mikka grunted. "Okay, that is a good use for coffee. And we don't have half these spices anyway."

Together we assembled the rest of the empanadas and put them in the oven.

As I put the fry pan and mixing bowl in the sonic cleaner, my repair worries knotted my stomach. "I need to look at that front skid again. The printer should be done by now, and we have to get it fixed or we can't land."

Taking the coffee and another biscotti, I headed aft through the common room and down the ladder, with Mikka following along. The mechanism for the front skid was out under the bridge and sealed by the outer hull. It was outside, so I'd sent my one, small, diagnostic robot out to map the damage. The weird physics of Lu space seemed to confuse it, and it took days just to get out there.

In the meantime, I'd cut one of the cargo bay ceiling panels to form into a new skid and started printing up replacement parts. I just had to figure out how to install the thing outside the ship in Lu space.

Going over to the engineering station by the rear wall across from the ladder, I found the robot's scans and swiped them up onto the wall, both digital scans and videos.

As I turned the images, I sighed. The bay doors were scratched and dented. The skid itself was gone. The struts and hydraulics had been mangled. Oil had sprayed everywhere before the automatic sealants had stopped the leaks.

The printer had stopped making noise, meaning it had finished. I swiped the skid schematics up onto a different section of wall so we could see it while doing the assembly.

Mikka helped me get the hydraulics and the structural parts out of the printer tray. She held one up and laughed. "These printers saved our lives when we first arrived on Eksil, but this one is fjern more advanced than what we have."

I hadn't thought of that. A 3D printer, especially a big one, when first landing on a planet, would be invaluable. That is, if they had a good set of plans to go with it or a way to customize what they had.

I picked up one of the hydraulic hoses and connected it to the new strut. "Let's hope mine is as useful as yours."

Following the schematics, we assembled the strut, but I started getting a bad feeling as I saw it go together. At last, I grabbed the rear strut and took it over to the robot's image on the wall. The broken assembly had three bolts and a side brace. The one in my hand had four bolts and no brace.

Swearing, I tossed the new strut to the deck and searched the computer for diagrams of the new design. I didn't find any. "Damn it, Earl. You're going to pay for these repairs."

"Who is this Earl?"

I could probably fabricate the part the strut connected to. To see, I checked the scan the robot had done. A conduit now ran through the spot where the extra bolt would have gone.

I rubbed my neck. "He's my starship mechanic, the best. Although apparently not the best at documentation."

With a frown, I changed the scan on the wall to real size and held up the newly printed one next to it. Could I modify the schematic file to print the current, modified strut? Side by side, though, Earl's strut was larger and sturdier, so just modifying the head would not do it. How much mass did the changes we'd made add? It couldn't be that much.

Mikka stepped up behind me and looked over my shoulder. "Does it have to retract?"

I glanced at her, thinking. Leaving it extended would hurt aerodynamics, but our atmospheric entry at Earth should be tame enough. It would make landing a little rough, but I could compensate. Was the Lu-space bubble wall far enough away from the ship to put the skid out there?

Turning, I sat on the floor and brought telemetry up on the wall. The gravity field formed an elliptical lozenge around the ship, meaning it was closest at sides, front, and back, and farther away at top and bottom. Thus, if I kept the skid a little rearward of its usual position, it should be fine.

I got to my feet and hugged Mikka. "Not retracting it should be enough to get us on the ground."

Going over to the engineering station at the rear, I brought up my design software and opened the strut assembly. I just erased the existing struts altogether and started building an angled truss that I could weld to the Revenge's frame.

An hour later, I had the plans. Mikka had brought more coffee for me, and I sipped the hot brew. My design had three pyramid-shape trusses that descended to stiff joints, below which were three smaller pyramids that attached to a new V-shaped skid that had its own stiff hinge. The structure could take twice the *Revenge's* total weight. If I didn't land too hard or fall from twenty meters, it would hold.

All we had to do was build it in a single day. And figure out how to install it outside the ship.

Mikka touched my shoulder. "The empanadas are ready. Let's go eat."

I set the printer to make the parts and we headed up. After gathering water, plates, napkins, and empanadas in the galley, Mikka and I went out to the common room, sat at the little table, and ate. I didn't say anything as I tried to figure out how to get my new apparatus installed.

Mikka took a long pull on her water after eating an entire empanada. "Whoo! Such spices! The skid has to go outside the ship? If we were on the ground, could you get to it from inside?"

Elbows on the table, eating two-handed, I had to resist rolling my eyes. She really didn't know how this stuff worked. "Yes, but there's air on the ground. We have to go through the inner and outer hull to get to it."

She paused before taking a bite, empanada right at her mouth, and grinned. "What if we let the air back out into this Lu space again?"

I opened my mouth to refute her assertion, then closed it again. We were trained, drilled, to never breach the inner hull in flight, let alone the outer. But we'd had air filling the whole pocket universe already. We could fill it up again.

"And here I thought we were done breaking rules on this flight."

★★★★★

Sixteen hours later, Mikka and I flopped down into the pilot and copilot seats and sealed the bridge. My body fairly melted into the smart foam. After lifting, assembling, and manhandling that skid, my bones felt wearier than I'd ever been. Even basic training back at the academy hadn't been this bad, or this long.

Forcing my arms to move, I donned my flight helmet and jacked in, then brought up the life support telemetry in my Virtual Vision. A red flashing light told me the airlock was open. The fallout timer clicked under four hours until we arrived at Earth.

We'd been flying with the back door open for the entire time. Every time I broke those concrete rules, I shuddered. But I did it. We had to rig a wire harness to hold struts and skids in place while we brought in other parts.

But it had worked. We'd taken apart the inner and outer hulls and installed the strut from inside the ship.

Now, with the skid in place and the hulls sealed again, I set life support to vacuum in the entire ship except the bridge.

"Well, it shouldn't take more than an hour to get all the air back inside. Then we can close the airlock."

I sat watching the air pressure gauge, waiting.

The fallout alarm went off. I jerked awake. The drive cut off and I floated. The amorphous colors around us stretched and brightened. The red airlock light still flashed.

I swore. "Computer, emergency close airlock!"

Mikka stirred, waking.

Then I realized the airlock being open didn't matter. We were in clear space and the rest of the ship, other than the bridge, was already in vacuum.

I forced my body to relax. My eyes were scratchy.

"What's wrong?" Mikka asked, sounding sleepy.

I had to take a deep breath to convince my body that there wasn't an emergency. "Nothing. We left the back door open while we slept, but no burglars got in. And...we're here. Welcome to Sol system."

I looked out at what my Virtual Vision showed me; it magnified the salient features. Straight ahead, a sliver of blue was all that marked Earth, and it was still small. Standard approaches were from about the moon's orbit. The moon, a silver quarter-circle, lay off to the right. The sun was a tiny yellow disk on the left.

Having not been back since my brief transits on the liners going to and from New Zion and Solomon Tech, I took the time to breathe in the sight. There was just something about coming here, where humanity started. While there was a diaspora going on, more people still lived here than on all the colony worlds combined.

Mikka stirred in her seat and whispered. "For us, Earth is almost a legend."

It wasn't like most of us from the frontier got back here much either. What did I know about Earth? I gestured toward the planetary tableau. "You are about to see it for real."

I powered on my drives and set the life support back to normal.

Then I ran a little computer program that changed my transponder ID. It wasn't supposed to be possible, but I'd found a way. Two sets of hardware did it.

"We'd better prepare for landing, which means we have to forgo the view." I flipped the patched-together *Revenge* over to fly bottom first and started decelerating like any inbound ship.

Then I opened a channel to Armstrong Station and Sol System Flight Control. "This is *SS Shadow Wing* requesting landing clearance for North America." I transmitted the clearance protocol that Ghazi had included on his data crystal.

After waiting for the time lag, Armstrong answered with approval.

I shrugged. "And now we wait. When we get within a thousand kilometers, they'll take over the landing."

I didn't like giving up control, but this was Earth with thousands of ships landing and taking off from the surface every day, and thousands more doing the same at the space stations. My gravity scans and other sensors took in the surroundings. Four liners were in-system now, on their hyperbolic arcs off the ecliptic. The Council of Planets Navy had a base on the moon and their own space station in orbit, not to mention patrol ships at various points.

Three hours later, we had decelerated enough such that a normal ship couldn't jump out again without serious acceleration. My Virtual Vision highlighted a ship coming toward us. I did some course projections and found it got within a hundred kilometers, which was closer than ships usually came. It was also a high-g engine, likely making it a long-range courier or a jump fighter, but a fighter seemed unlikely.

I adjusted my course a little farther away. The oncoming ship didn't alter course to come closer. Still, I set my sensors, especially the telescopes, to monitor the courier. It passed by without incident and jumped not long after that.

I played back a close-up view of the courier, but it had no markings. None at all. That was unusual for a courier, since people like me couldn't even buy such ships. Still, it shouldn't have come so close. "I don't like that."

Mikka stirred and looked around. "What's wrong?"

I shook my head. "Probably nothing, but I think that ship may have been verifying that we're the ship from Eksil."

Mikka grunted. "I've been reading all the histories you have, everything on politics, even the movies and fiction peripherally related, and I still can't make sense of this. With all the colonies, there is no shortage of resources, why all the posturing and power plays? Don't you pick leaders for empathy and charisma?"

She kept asking such strange questions. "Well, different planets and regions on Earth choose leaders in different ways. Angel's planet, which is, well, not my home, but where I live, is owned by one person."

Mikka didn't answer for a while. "Hmm. We have so little experience of these things. I also do not know why you must hide your identity. Are people chasing you?"

I chuckled. "After a fashion, but they want to use me rather than harm me."

As Mikka started to ask something else, my radar beeped at me. Three more ships on intercept course, one launching from the moon. The radio buzzed.

Armstrong station control said, "*SS Shadow Wing*, stand to. There is a warrant for the arrest of all on board and the seizure of your ship."

9
EMERGENCY DESCENT

An arrest warrant for me? As we decelerated toward Earth, a chill went through me that ignited a fury. Only the Romans would know what my ship looked like, plus, they wanted my ship. This had to come from them. They were not getting my ship, not *Hiram's Revenge*. I would destroy it first.

I started to answer, but Mikka put a hand on my arm. "Am I not an ambassador? Does that not give me privilege?"

A smile grew on my face as I flipped the radio to respond. "Armstrong Control, this is *Shadow Wing*. We are an ambassadorial ship, and as such no warrants of any kind are valid."

Sweat ran down my back as we waited for a reply. This could go wrong in so many ways. It seemed to take longer than just a reply. Maybe they were conferring with someone.

At last, Armstrong replied. "*Shadow Wing*, you will surrender to authorities. Once you dock at Armstrong, we'll work this whole thing out."

Mikka let out a big breath. "What now? Is docking at Armstrong a good idea?"

I pursed my lips. "No, it is not. If I lose control of this ship, I'll never get it back. And you will be in their control, too."

"I don't want to be in anyone's control."

"Then we leave and make a new plan." I flipped the radio open. "Armstrong Control, as we said, you have no authority over this ship or anyone on it. We reject your request to dock at the station."

Before the message had time to get to the station, I whipped thrust from below the *Revenge* to out back. I punched it to four gs, at right angles to the direction we had been going,

It took the chase ships a few moments to respond. They'd also been lazy, all approaching on the ecliptic, which left me a hole to escape through. Still, they accelerated at five gs. They raced me to Lu space.

Two of them launched missiles.

"What are those tracks?" Mikka asked.

"Missiles. They're trying to prevent us from leaving."

Mikka stirred in her chair. "Humph. Perhaps we should reject their additional requests to remain."

I nodded. "Good plan."

Even so, I needed a little more energy. The missiles approached detonation range. They would be proximity bursts.

"Boost!"

The Revenge jumped forward. The missiles closed. The green jump light came on at last.

I hit the jump button. The stars, and Earth, stretched and faded away.

Once fully in Lu space, I brought us back to a reasonable three gs. Then I turned the *Revenge* toward Pluto, on the far side of the sun. I switched the transponder back to *Hiram's Revenge*. A minute later, we fell out again.

The light plume faded, leaving Pluto and Charon orbiting gray and cold thirty thousand kilometers above us. For the moment, I left the gravity drives off, so we floated, weightless.

Mikka stirred against her belts. "That did not go as well as hoped."

I pounded the console beside me. "No. And I'm not happy with my employers. They should have been able to prevent that entire thing."

Mikka sighed. "My enemies seem legion and my friends powerless."

I considered how I could get down to that North American site without being caught. Whatever I did, people on Earth

would know what I had done to the *Revenge*, or at least that
I'd done something to it.

Mikka, however, was not done. "I wish to float."

She unbuckled and pushed herself out of her seat.

I jacked out and removed my helmet in time to see her
run gently into the canopy and stay up there. She grimaced,
as if about to be sick. She probably was.

"You'd best come down."

I gave us a tenth of a g thrust. Mikka fell, slowly, to her
seat.

"Ugh. That was so not komfortabel. I do have a thought."
She squirmed around face up again and buckled her belts. "I
do want to veksling, um, change the plan. I would rather go to
the Council of Planets alone, on my own, without the
assistance of any faction."

The woman learned fast. She didn't want to be in
anyone's debt. Getting an audience, though, might be
difficult.

I frowned. "As long as I get paid for this mess."

Mikka turned to look in my eyes. "If these idioter refuse to
pay, come to Eksil. We will pay."

That was a generous offer, considering she had no idea
how much it would cost. There was also the issue of Eksil not
being on any interstellar monetary system.

I rubbed my neck, thinking about trying to get all the way
to the ground without being shot down. "I guess we're going to
Beijing. But we need a place where the public and the press
will see and hear you before we get arrested."

"How do we do that?"

"First, we get some sleep. Then we see if we can find some
tourists."

The next day, such as "day" was, I set us to half a g,
accelerating toward the sun. Then Mikka and I ate a nice
breakfast of something called Øllebrød, kind of a bread
pudding thing. It had an aftertaste I didn't appreciate, but it
was good overall, and someone else was cooking.

As we ate, I brought up the system-wide ship's registry.
With relays throughout Sol system, it showed every ship,
though some were many hours old. We were only looking for
ones near Pluto.

There were three comet miners, four science vessels, one luxury yacht, and a touring ship from New Zion. At least that part was easy.

"Computer, open a channel to the *Bruxim Hashavim*."

The computer beeped and a voice came on. "Hello, *Hiram's Revenge*. This is Ensign David of the *Bruxim Hashavim*, how may I help you?"

"Greetings, Ensign. I'm Captain Hannah. Would you happen to have the Earth entertainment database for this week? My passenger is a bit eccentric and we're taking an inbound charter. Didn't have time to pick up any info."

"That data costs us a subscription. You can get your own. The channel I will send."

Signing up would likely give us away and take hours.

I could offer to pay, but I'd learned a few things at Solomon Tech. "You know how it is, impatient tourists. It's been a while since I was on New Zion. You ever go to Goldblum's Flying Circus in New Hebron?"

"Goldblum's! First thing I ever flew! Did you hear about the girl who stole one of his planes and buzzed the Solomon Tech graduation?"

I winced. That had been me, of course. "No! How is that possible?"

"I have no idea. Some rumor about a screwdriver. Goldblum got in a lot of trouble over it, though."

My computer beeped, warning me of an incoming data stream. I accepted it.

I shook my head in sympathy for Goldblum. I hadn't meant to get him in trouble, but I had needed to find out what the bastards would let me get away with. "I miss those simpler times. Wish I could go flying there now."

"You make me sick for home. Don't let the tourists get you down. Shalom."

"Shalom, my friend."

I broke the connection, smirking at the strangeness of the world.

Mikka cocked her head. "You were the one who did that thing at graduation?"

The woman paid attention. I could lie to her, but she'd know I was lying, and I wanted her trust. "Knowing that, you could figure out who I am."

Reaching across the little table, Mikka laid a hand on mine. "You have hjælped me more than you needed. I will not røbe, um, betray you."

"Thank you."

I swiped the entertainment database onto the wall. Using a projected virtual keyboard, I searched for Beijing events tomorrow. There were thousands. I amended the search for outdoor venues. There were still hundreds. I started scrolling through the list. One big problem was knowing which ones were big enough for me to land.

Mikka stood, looking at the list. "Vente. Go back."

I scrolled back up a bit, and Mikka pointed at one line. "What is that?"

There was a Panda Festival at a place called the Forbidden City. That sparked something from my Earth history classes long ago.

"Computer, show me more about the Forbidden City. Include pictures."

An image of an old Chinese building, low and wide, with big courtyards appeared. It had been the imperial palace long ago. The festival was in a courtyard in front of the Hall of Supreme Harmony.

I whistled. "An ambassador from a lost colony could possibly be confused that this is still the real palace. It's perfect."

Then the reality sank in. Ships falling out of Lu space too close would be fired on. No one wanted a repeat of the raid on the shipyards from the war where Roman Destroyers fell out, dropped nukes, and jumped again. That meant I would have to fall out awfully close and get into the atmosphere. And my new front strut did not have heat shielding.

I got up and paced. "Well, we're going to wish we had that laser cannon, and I have to go outside to make more repairs. Going down hard through an atmosphere is why we want retractable skids."

"Oh, dear. And I suggested making it not retract."

Laying a hand on her shoulder, I forced a smile. "We had to have a skid. Now we do. I just have to figure out how to keep it."

An hour later, I'd started the printer making more missile-defense chaff. I had some, but more would be good for this landing. Mikka was strapped in on the bridge, and I had my pressure suit on. I carried the hull-repair kit with extra foam modules in my pockets as I floated into the airlock. You couldn't go EVA under thrust.

The inner door closed behind me. I hooked my tether to the loop in the airlock wall while I waited for the air to cycle out. Then I got the EVA drone out of the compartment and hooked it to a loop in my belt.

The airlock beeped in my intercom and the outer door unlocked. At least we weren't flying with the door open now. This was, if not normal, at least reasonable. I cranked the handle and braced against the inside door to slide the outer one open. The door receded into the wall.

I dove out the door headfirst, upside down from the *Revenge's* point of view. Catching the ladder on the way down, I pulled myself along. Pluto had receded some, but its gray disk still lent contrast to the myriad stars all around. The Milky Way smeared across the heavens. Out here, the sun could barely be distinguished from any other star.

When I reached the bottom of the *Revenge,* I pulled myself up until my head cleared the ship and I could see the front skid. Then I grabbed the drone, without unhooking it from my belt. Its tether played out. I aimed it toward the skid and powered it on.

I gave it the go command. It zipped away from me, giving me a little kick backward as it did. Fortunately, I was holding onto the last rung.

The drone got to the new skid and latched on. I launched myself off the ladder and hit the button on the hook. The drone reeled me in. I flew through space beneath my ship.

When I got to the skid, my tether still hooked onto the airlock jerked me to a stop. Then came the boring part; manually forming the lattice around all the parts of skid and strut, forming a barrier angled to prevent the bay itself from sustaining damage. I spread the goo and cured it with the wand. It took almost two hours, but I finally finished.

Detaching the drone, I turned it off. Then I put my feet on the *Revenge* and jumped. The tether swung me out and away.

"Wooo-eeee!"

Mikka laughed in my ear. I hit the button on my suit and the tether reeled me back in. My momentum swung me out and around, and I watched the stars flow by as I swung all the way around. I landed feet first on Revenge's aft hull, above the airlock.

Wishing that I could take the time to do that swing again, I instead hopped into the airlock and closed the outer door.

Moments later, after the airlock filled again, I floated into the *Revenge*, down the hall, and onto the bridge.

Mikka looked up from Hiram's seat and smiled. "You're good at this zero-g living."

I flipped into the pilot's seat and shrugged. "Zero-g gymnastics back in school." That seemed like two lifetimes ago now.

After buckling in, I donned my helmet, jacked in, and powered up the drives.

"You think that will hold?" Mikka asked.

I charted a course back to Earth, checked the local time in Beijing, and accelerated inward.

I flexed my hands on the joysticks. "If not, landing will be interesting."

We both got up then and changed clothes. No flight suit for me this time. Mikka had given me a pair of silver epaulets and two silver pins with gold, silver, and red stones. I put them on a black dress shirt and donned matching dress pants. They were salvaged from my academy dress uniform. Then I added a black stocking cap that my parents Jo and Jeffers had given me long ago, with my hair tucked underneath. The wrap-around shades I carried back to the bridge.

Mikka emerged from her room and stepped onto the bridge wearing a gold-lame jacket with no collar over a violet blouse and matching pants. She also had a three-stone pin on her shoulder.

I handed Mikka an earbud and microphone hooked to the *Revenge's* intercom, and together we strapped in, jacked in, and got ready.

I double-checked the course, which included a descent in Lu space, so I'd have a boost available. The first jump was, as with my approach to Eksil, to get us lined up and at the right angle for our planned approach. I could have turned in Lu space, but taking the time to plot the course precisely was better.

I hit the jump button. The stars stretched and faded. I changed the ship's registry again. A minute later the colors brightened and reappeared. I'd set us up five light minutes out.

As we floated, my navigation computer plotted a course to Beijing, coming in low and fast, west to east so we'd be over land, populated country. I hoped that would make them hesitate to rain missiles down on us.

"When we fall out, get on the radio and broadcast that you're a diplomat from Eksil. Say it in Danish, English, and any other languages you know."

I pressed the pedal down and accelerated us toward Earth. "You ready for this?"

Mikka snorted. "No, but I have little choice."

I hit the jump button. The stars stretched, faded, and reappeared. The blue disk of Earth loomed below us.

I tipped the *Revenge's* nose down, heading for the stratosphere.

It took mere seconds for us to get an emergency abort message. Mikka answered in a language I did not know.

The *Revenge* bucked when it hit the stratosphere. I struggled to keep the nose at the right angle, then accelerated into a steep dive. Suddenly the whole thing reminded me of evading a Roman blockade. This time I couldn't hide in the dark, though.

Three destroyers broke orbit, heading down. A dozen fighters scrambled from Armstrong Station.

The *Revenge* left a trail of flame and white smoke. We crossed from the Caspian Sea over the desert. Missiles launched out of Punjab Province and Tashkent.

From above, the destroyers fired two missiles each. Six more fighters launched out of a base near Shanghai. Commercial traffic began rerouting away from my path.

Mikka squirmed in her seat. "They appear to be serious about shooting us down."

Sweat was forming under my arms and down my back. "You'd think they don't like us."

I banked right, away from the Tashkent missiles, which were the closest. Wishing I had another decoy missile, I tipped the *Revenge's* nose down. I needed to lose altitude before I showed off the *Revenge's* abilities.

The missiles closed in. How long could I wait before launching chaff?

We crossed thirty-thousand meters altitude. I put us into a steeper dive. Then I plotted a jump-course to Beijing where I fell out with engines active.

Would they use proximity bursts this close to the ground? How far down did they assume I could get before the missiles caught me?

Mikka pointed toward the rear. "Those missiles are getting close."

I hit the boost. We shot forward at over five gs. Missiles still closed, from above and behind on both sides. "We have to let them think they're winning."

Mikka snorted. "Aren't they?"

I banked left, trying to get all the missiles to arrive at once. "Well, yes. So far."

We passed twenty thousand meters. I needed to get under ten.

Fifteen thousand.

The missiles reached five kilometers. Fighters above and in front reached a hundred kilometers, almost targeting range.

Four, three, two...

I released chaff. Then I pulled out of the dive. That slowed us down. The missiles got within a kilometer.

I hit the jump button.

10
FORBIDDEN CITY

The Earth below us stretched and faded. Then it reappeared with a bang.

Beijing spread for kilometers. A thunderstorm gathered to the north and the ocean stretched blue and flat into the distance.

A shockwave spread out from *Hiram's Revenge*, a gale-force wind. I decelerated hard, using the boost.

I'd angled the course down, so we fell out at less than two thousand meters. I just hoped the sunlight would hide the light plume and confuse the CPN ships long enough for us to get down.

Local traffic control yelled in my ear.

I opened a channel. "Sorry, sorry, I'm coming down. Diplomatic mission."

I did just that, dropping as fast as I dared. At five hundred meters I started dodging buses and grav-cars.

Mikka pointed. "There it is!"

The rectangular moat surrounding the Forbidden City glittered in the sunlight. The red and gold wall rose a few meters high beyond the water. It stretched almost a kilometer north to south.

Mikka said, "That's an imponerende palace."

I brought the *Revenge* down to a hundred meters and slowed us way down, but still going too fast for local traffic. Beijing traffic police closed in on our position, but they weren't equipped to handle something the size of the *Revenge*.

More fighters appeared, coming in high from the south, likely from Shanghai again. The CPN had found us. They appeared to be cutting us off from getting to the Council of Planets Government Complex, which was on a man-made island in the bay.

Going there would have been suicide. Landing at all might be suicide.

With a dozen traffic police grav cars around us, I brought the *Revenge* to a screaming halt fifty meters over the far wall, the east wall, of the Forbidden City. With deliberate care, I dropped down even more and headed back for the big courtyard before the Hall of Supreme Harmony with its grand stair and tiered wall.

Five hundred people stared up at the *Revenge*. When I started down, they scattered. I gave them time to get out of the way. The police cars squawked, telling us it was forbidden to land there, and any damage would lead to arrests.

I landed anyway, setting down as gentle as a feather. I shut the engines down.

Mikka and I scrambled to get our straps unbuckled and helmets off. We dashed to the back. Mikka grabbed one of her bags on the way by her room. We fairly slid down the ladder to the cargo deck. There, we stepped out onto the ramp, and I used my brace to start lowering it. That way we would appear right at the bottom and would not have to walk down.

Mikka lost her balance and waved her arms.

I caught her shoulder to steady her. She managed not to move her feet.

The ramp seemed to take forever. I just hoped no one would shoot us before Mikka could talk. Would the Romans have an agent in the crowd? How would they have known to come here?

I would rather have been dodging missiles.

Our feet and legs were exposed, then our torsos. At last, our heads cleared the bottom of the *Revenge,* and we could see out. A dozen security guards stood between us and the crowd, but they seemed uncertain whether to keep the crowd back or protect the crowd from us. Only two had weapons drawn, and they looked like stun guns. Being stunned now would still be a disaster.

Several hundred people had gathered close, eschewing the Panda Festival, finding a starship landing in the courtyard much more exciting. Behind them, there were booths and displays, places for food and more, but not a single panda except in pictures and videos. Were they extinct?

Above the general Beijing traffic, a dozen CPN fighters hovered. Police vehicles seemed to be landing, but outside the Forbidden City. I hoped the time it took them to get inside would be enough.

Tourists held up phones and computers to record us. A handful of reporters pushed to the front, also ready to record.

Four of the security guards moved toward us, looking angry.

Mikka raised her hands and spoke, her voice amplified by the *Revenge's* speakers. "I am Ambassador Mikka Retts of the planet Eksil!" She gestured around her. "I declare this ground, and this ship my embassy, sovereign territory of Eksil. Let none enter without my permission."

The four security guards stopped short. They clearly didn't have the training to deal with this but knew what an embassy was. The crowd murmured in excitement. The reporters spoke into their microphones, and no one looked away.

"I know that none of you have heard of Eksil. I am the first person from there to visit Earth since my ancestors immigrated on the *Sydney-Copenhagen*. We are most pleased to re-establish formal ties with Earth."

Exclamations of astonishment broke out from the crowd. The words echoed around the courtyard. There had been many lost ships since then, but none as spectacular, being as big as the ship was and as early as it was in human interstellar flight.

Two squads of police officers jogged into the courtyard. Cowing local security guards was one thing. Beijing police would be another. They started pushing through the crowd.

While some people deferred to the police, most resisted, and grew angry at the intrusion.

Mikka addressed the Panda Festival security guards, pointing at the oncoming police. "Stop them from invading my planet!"

Eight of the security guards turned and found themselves facing some rather angry Beijing Police, who tried to push on by.

The head Panda security guard, a wiry woman with gray hair, stood her ground. She held up a hand. "Stop! This is our jurisdiction. And that is an ambassador."

I leaned close to Mikka. "Impressive."

She winked and covered the mic. "I've been reading up."

When the Beijing police looked like they were going to push past the security guards, Mikka put hands on hips. "Let the leader of this planet come to me here or send his representative. No others may cross this line and come onto Eksil soil."

Two officers who'd come in with separate groups conferred. One turned away and got on the radio. The other waved her men back and stepped forward. "You have violated Earth airspace, landed without permission, endangered local air traffic and committed a dozen other offenses. I am placing you under arrest."

Mikka gave him a grave nod. "For these offenses, I apologize. I am unfamiliar with local laws and customs. However, your officials attempted to arrest me and confiscate my ship before hearing from my embassy. This I could not allow, so here we are." She spread her arms, waiting.

I rubbed my face to keep from smiling. The woman was good. Then again, Eksil probably sent their absolute best person for this assignment, considering the importance.

The crowd got into it then. "They're from the *Sydney-Copenhagen!*"

"Talk to the council!"

"Let her be heard!"

Mikka leaned over to me. "Do you have any chairs we could bring out here?"

"Sorry, no."

She winked at me and turned to the crowd, since the police seemed to be busy talking to their bosses. "Friends, there seems to be an oversight in the equipment on my ship. Would any of you have a pair of chairs we might borrow while we wait for the powers that be to decide on my embassy?"

Everyone laughed, but a couple of the vendors retrieved chairs for us. And then we waited. The police milled about. The crowds grew bored. Some of them went back to the panda exhibits.

One of the reporters braved the police line, raising a hand to wave. "Excuse, please. Might you some questions answer?"

"Of course." Mikka addressed the officers. "Can you allow the reporters to come to the foot of the ramp, please?"

I imagined what would happen if everyone found out where Eksil was. Thousands of people, hundreds of ships at least, would arrive. Even without the Roman blockade, I doubted Eksil was ready for so many people, maybe not for any people.

I leaned close to Mikka. "Don't give them any idea where Eksil is, not even how far. At least not until the Romans are dealt with."

Mikka glanced at me, eyes narrowed, then nodded once.

The reporter who had asked for the interview stepped up first, with a woman behind him holding a camera. The reporter gave a little bow. "Apologies. My language...is difficult. Eksil where?"

With a dazzling smile, Mikka waved at the sky. "Eksil is out there somewhere. I am no astronomer to tell you where."

A different woman asked, "Why have you come now?"

"The simple story is that an explorer found us and coming here to rejoin the rest of humanity seemed prudent." Then Mikka frowned. "Since I am so unfamiliar with Earth, can you answer a question for me?"

A little surprised, the reporters agreed.

Mikka offered a self-deprecating grin. "Assuming the Council agrees to hear me, will they send just par people or mange?"

For a moment, the reporters all looked confused. After spending a month with Mikka, I had a guess. At last, a person with a camera said, "They will send many, a committee."

"Thank you." Mikka winked at the first man who did not know English. "I am unfamiliar, too." Then she frowned. "I am in need of a bord, um, table. Who is the arranger of this panda festival?"

Several reporters pointed at a woman moving from booth to booth talking to the vendors. The reporter who'd had issues with English ran and got the woman.

Mikka leaned over to me. "Will we need to pay for such a bord?

"I assume so. I will pay. Or my employers will, eventually."

The arranger, when asked, brought us eight chairs, and a table with a red tablecloth trimmed with gold patterns that looked like Chinese writing. Not long after that, four grav-limousines approached, circled once, and settled to the ground outside the Forbidden City.

Shortly, three women and four men strode in, surrounded by another half-dozen guards. More reporters followed them. Word had spread.

Mikka stood and greeted the entourage at the foot of the ramp. "Welcome to the embassy of the planet Eksil. The seven of you are welcome inside. Your guards are not. They will stay out here."

When the dignitaries and guards both started to object, Mikka raised a hand to forestall them. "This is not negotiable. This embassy has a staff of two. However, we will only be at the top of the ramp, and the ramp will remain open."

The seven, who looked to be from different Earth nations, conferred. As they spoke, several more grav-cars landed, which attracted the dignitaries' attention. At that, they spoke with one of the guards and then agreed.

As we started up, I noticed the guards all stood facing outward. Who had come in those other limousines?

Mikka leaned close. "Stand behind me at the bord and look menacing."

She was in her element, and I was rapidly getting in over my head. I had some knowledge of how the Council of Planets worked, or at least allegedly worked. Besides that, I had nothing to offer Mikka.

I traipsed in after all the dignitaries.

Making her way to the seat at the far end of the table, Mikka gestured for all the others to be seated. I walked over and stood at Mikka's shoulder; arms folded. There, Mikka introduced herself again.

When the others introduced themselves, I realized who had come in those other cars. This first bunch included representatives from the Asian, European, American, and African blocs, plus three deputy ministers. Odd. Then again, if word went up from the Beijing police through channels, it would reach the Earth government before it reached the Council of Planets. And the three ministers would all represent the Asian bloc, since it remained preeminent, even if their official titles were all part of Earth's government.

I leaned down and whispered in Mikka's ear. "These are all from Earth. None of the other planets in the council."

Mikka gave me a tiny nod, her expression not changing a bit.

Pleasantries out of the way, the leading minister asked the one question that mattered. "How do we know you are who you say you are?"

Mikka reached down, picked up her bag, and set it on the red tablecloth. "Would the certified log of the *Sydney-Copenhagen* be sufficient?"

While the dignitaries murmured astonishment, Mikka pulled an old metal box from her bag. It looked shielded and had several access ports; an ancient ship's black box. Those were supposed to be write-only and nearly indestructible.

She looked up and handed me the box. "Do you have cables to plug this in?"

It must have weighed two kilos, heavy for a computer. As I headed for the engineering station, the representative from the Americas caught my eye and winked. He seemed quite pleased with himself.

My original landing site was in the Americas. Could their bloc be behind getting Mikka here? They would have the money.

The ranking minister gestured toward me. "We'll need to take that and have it examined, of course."

Mikka smiled. "Absolutely not. Any examinations will be done here in my embassy."

The dignitaries argued, but Mikka stayed firm.

Meanwhile, I set the black box on the engineering station desk and rummaged around in the storage in the wall beside the station and found my universal cable. I took the male end and held it against the black box port. Then I pushed the button on the connector. The light came on and it probed the port, extending receptors in until it found all the ones that worked.

While I waited, I started a search for an antiquities dealer who could validate the black box, figuring we'd want independent verification, just in case. I also started searching for a private security company.

The connector gave me one beep, meaning it had all the physical connections. Now it had to get the data versus power wires figured out. My computer popped up a screen asking what kind of device this was. I had to go well down through the menu of choices to find a black box. When I did, it only took a few moments for the connector to give me two beeps.

The black box data opened on my engineering station console, complete with the ancient Earth Space Administration logo. I swiped it up onto the wall behind Mikka.

The logo alone brought gasps from the assembled. A certificate adorned the bottom of the screen. While that could be faked, it could be verified easily, even at over two centuries old.

Mikka glanced over her shoulder, then addressed me. "I have not reviewed this log myself, but I believe you will find a navigation computer diagnostic run by the command staff around three-quarters of the way through the planned twenty-eight-year journey."

She had to have *reviewed* this at the least. At a guess, she knew key parts by heart. Probably every school kid on Eksil knew the story. Why lie?

Uncertain, I just pulled up the search menu. There had to be a search feature on a black box for a planned decades-long flight. I found the diagnostic request, exactly where she said.

When the diagnostic came up, it showed hardware errors in the main processing chip. Did they not run parallel computing for navigation?

"Wait..." I went back to the beginning and found the original course settings, where they'd been headed and put that up beside the diagnostic. Then I walked over to get a closer look. "They were headed for Thurman, but the error had them at least thirty degrees off course from the start. No one looked outside to check?"

One of the dignitaries stood to take a closer look. "How did they get to any planet at all?"

Now I understood why Mikka had lied. She wanted me to have this reaction. So, what would I have done if I'd been captain? I looked at the dignitaries. "If it was me, I would have tried to find the closest star system of any kind in the general direction I was headed and go there."

A hubbub broke out in the courtyard below.

Mikka glanced down, then turned to the lead minister. "Has someone else come to visit my embassy?"

"No one that matters at the moment."

Rising from the seat at the table, Mikka headed down. "Oh, let's go see. I'm so new here that I want to meet everyone."

11
GUARDING THE EMBASSY

Standing at the upper end of the *Revenge's* cargo hold, I watched as the seven representatives of the Earth government hurried down the ramp after Mikka. They didn't want her meeting the representatives from the other planets alone.

I followed a little slower, making sure no one stayed behind.

At the bottom of the ramp, the Earth dignitaries' guards, along with some Beijing police officers, held back seven other dignitaries. As soon as the Earthers came into view, the newcomers started accusing them of grandstanding and shutting out the other planets.

Based on the badges on their coats, this group encompassed all the other council planets; Thurman, Nova Roma, Byzantium, which was a Roman colony, New Zion, Greenwood, New Serengeti, and Shang Du.

The reporters—who seemed to have multiplied—ate it up.

The Panda crowd, who had started drifting toward the exhibits, hurried back. More tourists and locals dashed in from all the entrances to the courtyard. Mikka was the main attraction in Beijing today.

Mikka let the various dignitaries argue for a bit. Then she leaned closer to me. "We're about to need evidence of the Roman blockade. Do you have anything you can show?"

The *Revenge's* sensor logs would certainly have such information. I would just need time to get it together.

I nodded. "I'll work on it. When we get up there again, keep them busy with the *Sydney-Copenhagen* logs for a while."

She laid a hand on my arm. "Thank you for your hjælp." Then she glanced at the arguing dignitaries and cocked her head. "Do you suppose I should stop them?"

"We could see if they come to blows first."

Mikka winked. "I have something better. Which one is from Nova Roma?"

I pointed with my chin. "The one with the laurel-leaf emblem. The one next to him is from Byzantium, a Roman colony."

Mikka strode forward and waved to encompass all the newcomers. "Excuse me. You are from the other planets in the council ting?"

All seven of them acknowledged that, vehemently.

"Good." She turned to the Earth representatives. "I believe we are through here. One of you should stay. The others should go back and report what you saw to your superiors. Arrange what tests you wish to do for the black box here in my embassy."

Mikka turned her attention back to the planetary representatives, then pointed at the ones from Nova Roma and Byzantium. "All of you, except the two of you, are welcome in my embassy. Come."

She started to turn away, but the Roman representative put hands on hips. "Why are we being excluded? We are full Council of Planets members!"

Mikka whirled on him. "But I am *not*, and this is the embassy from Eksil. You know why you are not welcome here. Remove your ships and we will talk."

With that, she spun on her heel and strode up the ramp. Apparently, the guards paid attention, as they let the five other planetary representatives through. One of the Earth representatives, not the senior one, also followed Mikka up.

At the table, Mikka picked up something that hadn't been there before, from the spot where the Americas representative had been sitting.

When I reached the top, I made a one-eighty to go to the engineering station. While Mikka got everyone seated and started over on the *Sydney-Copenhagen* black box, I brought up the sensor logs.

I started with what I'd seen once I cleared the gas giant. I zoomed in to remove most of the stars in the background. The view showed the number of ships in orbit. Then I skipped to what my ship saw at fallout. I had been paying attention to other things at that point.

Within range, there had been a Roman battleship, a carrier, and several destroyers. I froze the action, not showing how the *Revenge* was moving or where it was going. The Romans, helpfully, hadn't bothered to disable their transponders.

I stood and waved at Mikka. She nodded, so I swiped my little presentation up to the wall.

Mikka gazed at it for a moment, then turned back to the audience. "I did not invite the Nova Roma representative in because of that." She pointed back at the screen.

I walked forward. "This is my reconnaissance before I went in to pick up Ambassador Retts. You can see the number of ships around Eksil. When I got closer, I found this."

The next image showed, with extreme magnification, the Roman battleship *Nero*. The one after that, the carrier *Alexandria*. Another montage showed the destroyers. The presentation stopped on a squadron of fighters, all with clear Roman markings.

Mikka slammed her palm down on the table. "The Romans invaded my planet. I need *you* to make them go away!"

"Help we will," said the New Serengeti representative.

"As will we," answered New Zion.

The Earth representative raised a hand. "This has yet to be determined. The Romans are claiming you are their colony. All things in their time."

Mikka nearly lost her temper, but I raised a hand to stop her from saying anything. "May I suggest sending a delegation to Eksil? If that black box is not enough, send people. If they are a Roman colony, nothing on that planet will be older than fifty years old, seventy-five at most. If anything is older, they are not a colony."

Mikka gestured at the big metal box over at the engineering station. "But the black box should be sufficient. Still, if you have old DNA records, there is one other thing. I am a direct descendant of the first officer on the *Sydney-Copenhagen*."

I wondered if everyone on Eksil knew their ancestry that way. They certainly might.

The Earth representative frowned, not looking at all happy. "I would have to check. Such records might or might not be available." She stood. "However, we have enough information for the time being. We will let you know the Council's ruling on your embassy."

Mikka rose and reached out to shake hands with each dignitary and looked each in the eye. "Thank you all. I will await your decision, soon. I expect you to choose the side of truth."

When they'd all left, Mikka sighed and sank down into the nearest chair. "Is that it? What happens next?"

All I wanted to do was fly away, not play politics with the bastards who created me, but that wasn't what my customer needed. Some of what Brandy went through, how much she hated being the hero on display, echoed through the crowds outside.

I pointed down the ramp. "You have an audience out there, with reporters. Go talk to them. When it gets dark, we button up this ship and wait for the council to contact us."

What would the Romans next move be? What could I do to protect Mikka? Whatever it was, we were going to need help. As I'd suspected, we needed to hire local people, local security people.

Mikka distracted me by dragging me back down the ramp. She smiled and spread her arms to the crowd and the reporters. "We, on Eksil, tell many stories of our journey there. I suspect most have been embellished over the years."

One reporter shouted out; "What are the best ones?"

Mikka spread her hands. "I will tell it as my daughter did in her school play." She struck a pose, one arm raised like an orator. "Far into its long journey, the mighty *Sydney-Copenhagen* had turned and had been decelerating for two years. Passengers, looking out at the path of their glorious journey, saw no star getting closer, no destination approaching. Thus, on the worst day of the voyage, the navigator gathered the entire crew on the bridge. He stood before them, trembling in fear, and said, 'The reason Tau Ceti is not growing in our view screens is we are not headed toward Tau Ceti. We are light years off course.'

"Despair fell upon the people, and they cried out, 'Sorrow and woe! We are lost! Doomed to fly through the dark forever and ever!' But Captain Alinta, shortest in stature and tallest in wisdom, stood forth. 'Fear not! For our people are courageous and the dream time is strong.' The captain pointed overhead at a star in the distance, saying. 'The song lines lead there. We will journey to that star. And there we will forge a home for ourselves amid the light and boiling seas.' And such was her dreaming that this was exactly what happened."

Mikka took a bow as the reporters and tourists all cheered.

When the applause subsided, one of the reporters asked. "Why have you come here now and what does it have to do with the Romans?"

Taking a long breath, Mikka thought a moment before answering. "The Romans were the first people with, um, what was that?" She turned to me.

"Lu space."

"Ret." She turned back to the crowd. "They were the first people with Lu-space ships to finde us. Now, they are claiming we are their colony. I kom to stop them. And now, I need sleep." She smiled and waved as she turned away.

Some of the reporters wanted more.

Mikka bowed. "That is enough for tonight. Tomorrow, I will regale you with stories of what happened when the *Sydney-Copenhagen* arrived at Eksil."

We walked up the ramp, and I closed it using my bracer— starting it up before we reached the cargo bay, to reverse our earlier appearance.

Mikka shook herself out, then winked at me. "Thank you. You were very nyttig. Let's varm up some empanadas."

When we'd climbed the ladder and made our way from the common room to the galley, Mikka pulled a data crystal from her pocket. "I believe the representative from the Americas left this for you."

"Hmm. I suspect they hired me, and this should be payment."

Taking the crystal, I set up an isolated virtual computer and connected it to the port there in the galley. I slipped the crystal in. There were two files. One had private contact information. The other came up with my own certified encryption. I checked the contents, but left it encrypted; a bank draft for one million credits, plus twenty thousand for arriving two days early.

Joy welled up in my chest. That was enough money to even keep the bastards at bay, at least for a while.

The feeling faded, though. I still had to get out of here. I flipped the wall screen to the overhead view. That squadron of fighters was still hovering above us.

Mikka had warmed up the empanadas while I was investigating the crystal, so we trooped back to the common room. There we sat at the little table.

I took a bite, deep in thought. "What is the Roman's next move?"

12
VALIDATION

The following afternoon, Mikka stood on the Revenge's cargo ramp and regaled the crowd, now mostly tourists and visitors, with stories of trying to survive on a planet with little dirt and no night. They'd even tried to print soil on the 3D printers they were using to build shelters.

Then, a little old man with black glasses and white hair walked slowly to the front of the crowd and waited patiently for Mikka to finish. From the photo on his site, this was the antiquities dealer I'd hired.

Shortly after that, a bald person walked up in a plain shirt and khaki pants. They reminded me of my parents, except for the perpetual scowl. The equipment bag that person carried made me think this was a scientist from the Council of Planets.

Last, as Mikka's story wound down, a woman about my height strode to the edge of the crowd then all the way around the ship before coming to parade rest at the edge. She had violet hair, wrap-around shades like mine, and a lumpy jacket that might be concealing any number of things. Violet-hair could have been an assassin, but I suspected she was from the security company I'd talked to, since it was called the Lavender Shield. An assassin would be subtler.

I doubted the Romans were going to send an assassin, though. They wanted to discredit Mikka, and her story was already out there. Killing her would make her more likely to be believed. Besides, they wanted my ship.

When Mikka finished with a bow and the applause died down, the bald scientist stepped forward. "Excuse me. I am Dr. Mao. The Council sent me to examine, um…" Mao checked a computer. "…a black box?"

The old man, with a wry smile, joined Mao and bowed. "I am Guang, and I am also here to examine this black box."

Mikka waved at the crowd. "I'm afraid I have boring ambassador business."

While Mikka led the other two up the ramp, I beckoned violet-hair.

She strode over. "I am Pinyin Zeng. You need security assistance?"

"I'm Deuce, and I do. Come."

I led Pinyin up the ramp. By the time I arrived, Mikka had the black box sitting on the table. Guang leaned over it, touching his glasses. Mao scraped some metal flakes off the box and put them in a piece of equipment. It looked like a spectrum analyzer. It probably did half a dozen other things, too.

Leaning close to Pinyin, I whispered. "For now, watch. We'll talk when they're done."

Pinyin leaned on the red-covered table to get a closer look. "What are they doing? They're acting like it's fine porcelain."

I had to resist smiling. "If it's what it appears to be, it may be the most valuable thing you have ever laid eyes on."

Pinyin pointed at it. "It's an archaic piece of junk!"

I just shrugged.

Guang turned the black box on its side and pointed out something. He spoke in Mandarin.

Mao answered in the same language and typed something into his computer. A moment later he grunted. "Yǐ yànzhèng"

Pinyin pursed her lips. "He verified something."

Guang must have heard her. He looked up and nodded. "Yes, all things match so far. There is one test remaining. One that cannot be forged that we know."

Mao pulled out another piece of equipment and attached a cable to the same port I'd used, although this one seemed designed for it. The black box beeped, and a light went on near the top. It hadn't done that when I'd plugged it in. It emitted a series of lights and sounds. Mao's equipment made a responding set of sounds.

Then the pitch changed to a buzz.

Guang's head came up and he lunged for the cable. Mao, faster, grabbed his hand.

Guang struggled against the younger Mao, speaking through clenched teeth. "He's trying to erase it!"

Pinyin launched herself over the table. She tackled Mao. Mikka dashed in and ripped the cabled out of the black box.

Mikka took Guang's hand. "Did he skade it?"

The old man shook his head. "Méiyǒu. I will check, but those were the preparatory sounds only. These are made nigh impossible to erase."

Despite his confident words, he pulled a device from his pocket and plugged it in, humming worriedly to himself.

Pinyin hauled Mao up, hands bound. She pushed Mao to the table, forcing the prisoner to bend over it.

Then Pinyin leaned down and growled in Mao's ear. "Why did you do that? Who paid you?"

"It wasn't me! *He* was trying to erase it!"

Mikka walked over and lifted Mao's chin from the table. "It was your device. Mr. Guang had not plugged anything into my property. So unless he hacked your equipment without touching it before we walked in here, that seems unlikely."

There were so many aspects to Mao's attempted sabotage that I didn't know where to go first, although one seemed obvious.

I laid a hand on the black box. "Mr. Guang, I assume that you are convinced this is the real black box from the *Sydney-Copenhagen*?"

Guang bowed. "Háo wú yíwèn. There is no doubt. It is also unharmed."

Mikka bowed to him, in the same fashion. "Takker dig. Xièxiè"

She'd been studying, and it paid off. Guang's eyes glittered in appreciation.

Pinyin slapped Mao on the back. "And what do we do with this traitor?"

"I'm not a traitor! This is a fake box! It must be destroyed!"

Pinyin rolled her eyes. "In over their head." Then she leaned down next to Mao's ear. "If you do a dastardly deed, own it. Accept the consequences or don't do it."

Did that mean we needed to worry about Pinyin being honest? Possibly. Then again, she'd helped without being asked and without being hired. Neither Mikka nor I were prepared for the political minefield in Beijing, though Mikka seemed to be fast on her feet, as it were.

I turned to Mikka and gestured at Mao. "You declared this ship to be the sovereign territory of Eksil. That means Eksil law applies. Or maybe *Sydney-Copenhagen* law. We can always take him up and space him."

Mikka looked shocked, but a smile played at Pinyin's mouth.

Recovering from my dark humor, Mikka folded her arms. "I wish to think about fit punishment for a bit."

I patted the black box again. "Mr. Guang, what would you say the value of this black box might be?"

He rubbed his chin. "It is hard to say. There are exactly eight of these to have ever existed, seven are in museums on their planet of destination. But the black box from the lost juggernaut? Five hundred million, at least, likely more, should one be so vulgar as to sell it."

Pinyin blanched.

Mikka inclined her head. "Xièxiè. We will need a document of certification, and you may be called to testify before the Council of Planets."

Guang's eyes widened. "The Council?" With a little shake he recovered and bowed again. "Of course, for an object of such importance, I would be honored."

"Very well," Mikka said, with another slight bow. "That is all for today. We will contact you."

When Guang had departed, I turned to Pinyin. "Tell me, what would you do with Mao here?"

Mao squirmed, but kept his mouth shut.

She smirked and slapped Mao's back. "Short of spacing him? Make him into a double-agent and send him back against whoever sent him."

"But it's just the two of us." Mikka said.

I held up a hand. "Well, we do have a friend or two. We can at least ask before we resort to the airlock."

As Mao struggled not to say anything, I walked over to the engineering terminal. I felt like I shouldn't trust anyone, for Mikka's sake. But we had to trust someone. Unless we did, we were just two people with no resources.

First, I closed the ramp. Then I typed an urgent message and sent it off to my employers.

When I finished, Mikka was just climbing back down the ladder. Since the black box was no longer on the table, I assumed she'd secured it on the upper deck.

"Mikka, watch Mao. Pinyin and I need to talk."

I headed for the ladder. Pinyin whispered in Mao's ear before following. When we emerged into the common room, I folded the table back into the floor and brought the couch out of the wall. Then I offered her a seat.

She leaned back and smiled, which softened her features a lot. "What can I do for you, Deuce?"

I joined her on the couch and gestured at our surroundings. "I want to hire you to protect me, Mikka, this ship, and that black box."

Pinyin snorted. "You're not asking much."

I liked this woman, so I started to get up. "If you can't handle it, I can find someone else."

She reached out and touched my hand. "Oh, the Lavender Shield can handle your needs."

Smiling, I sat back down. "I am wondering about moving the black box out of here. If we do that, we will need a bond. Maybe a billion credits against the loss of the black box."

Pinyin whistled and leaned back again. "A billion?"

I shrugged, knowing I was pushing hard. "It's not a replaceable item. That much should give the Lavender Shield sufficient motivation to protect it."

"Well, I will have to check with my insurance company. To the rest, I agree." She held out her hand. "I'll send over the actual contracts."

We shook hands. Her grip was firm, but she let her fingers lightly caress my palm on the way by.

Pinyin leaned forward. "One more question. Am I working for you?"

That was a good question. I was the one with money. I rubbed my neck, wishing I could fly away. "I handle the money at the moment, but I work for Mikka, so you work for her."

A smile bloomed on her face. "Oh, good. That leaves other possibilities."

What possibilities did she mean? I wasn't sure I wanted to know. I snorted. "The possibility I want is for this to be over so I can fly away and go back to anonymity."

Pinyin leaned back, smile getting bigger. "You're just an adrenaline junkie."

I folded my arms. "And you aren't?"

She pointed a thumb at the ladder. "If we want excitement, we can get Mao and have a threesome."

I broke up laughing.

★★★★★

An hour later, two men showed up and asked for entry. We were sitting around the table in the cargo hold eating cashew chicken and steamed rice that Pinyin had ordered for us.

I got up to open the ramp, but Pinyin grabbed my arm to stop me. "It's my job to open the door now."

Rather than going for the ramp controls, she headed up the ladder and into the rear airlock. I followed, mostly because I didn't want a stranger, even one I'd hired, unescorted in my ship. But the feeling of uselessness increased. If Mikka had Pinyin, why did she need me?

While Pinyin closed the inner door and opened the outer, I brought the airlock camera up so I could see and hear what she was saying. While we were eating, it started raining. Menacing clouds hung low enough over the city that it obscured the CPN fighters above us.

Outside, a man and a woman, both hulking, stood in the rain looking up.

When the door receded into the wall, Pinyin leaned out. "Hello. Who are you and what do you want?"

The soaked woman scowled. "We're here, um, to pick up, well, an intruder."

Deuce's Exile – 95

Pinyin scowled right back. "Show me your credentials."

Both visitors held up badges that had electronic emitters.

Pinyin did something with her glasses and nodded. "We'll be right down."

She closed the outer airlock door and opened the inner, letting in the smell of rain and damp stone. She nodded back toward the visitors. "You have interesting friends. They're America's Coalition Secret Service. Do we give Mao to them?"

We didn't have anyone else to give him to. I shrugged. "At this point, anything to get rid of Mao."

Pinyin chuckled and turned to head down the ladder. "Good point. I just wish my team would get here."

I followed her down. "I did send *my* message out first."

In the cargo hold, Pinyin walked over to Mao, but addressed Mikka. "Ambassador, I would feel better if you were above decks with the hatch closed."

Mikka started to object but thought better of arguing with the one person who knew what might happen down here. The ambassador climbed the ladder and closed the hatch at the top.

Meanwhile, I lowered the ramp while Pinyon glared at Mao and picked up their equipment bag. "Get up. You're leaving."

I folded my arms but had to resist grinning. "And not out the airlock."

Together, the three of us stepped over to stand on the ramp as it lowered.

I looked over at Pinyin as we made our appearance. "You know, I usually get in and out of my ship through the airlock like a normal person."

Pinyin, winked at me. "You? Normal? I think not."

When the ramp got down, the two agents stepped under the ship's overhang, both scowling and grumpy, not to mention soaked. A few tourists with umbrellas hurried toward the Hall of Supreme Harmony, but no one waited outside to hear Mikka's stories today.

I pushed Mao forward. "This scientist attempted to destroy the *Sydney-Copenhagen* black box. Thus, I assume, the Romans paid them off. What you do with them now is not my concern, although verifying where the orders came from would be good."

The male agent took possession of Mao, while the woman folded her arms and glared at me. "We would have been happy to provide security for the ambassador."

Even though she could likely break me in two, I stepped up to her and looked into her eyes. "Who do you work for?"

"The Americas Coalition, of course."

I sneered and pointed a thumb at Pinyin. "That's the reason. *She* works for the ambassador."

The agent poked my chest. "We'd still protect you better than this mercenary."

With a huff, she turned and yanked Mao out into the rain.

The male agent handed me a data crystal, but he didn't look any happier than the woman. "We're very good at our jobs."

I nodded to him. "I would assume excellent."

Pinyin watched as they left, then pointed with her chin toward the south entrance. "I *am* a mercenary. But I hired my team. I gave them jobs, and I will do anything to support their families. That means staying in business, which in turn means never betraying a trust and being exceptionally good at my job."

I had not asked, but it made sense, and that she felt the need to say something mattered. It increased my trust in her.

In the direction she'd pointed, a dozen people strode in, almost marching, in two columns of six and carrying lavender umbrellas with large L's on them. Each one appeared unlike the next, even from a distance; tall, short, wide, thin, and some wild hair colors: one green, one pink, and three that matched Pinyin's. It looked like a couple shaved heads, too.

The two Americas agents had looked like they fit in, went together. These did not. When they got closer, one of Pinyin's had silver hair and wrinkles. At least one with a shaved head was older than Jeffers. Three weighed more than would be allowed in most military or police organizations.

The group marched right up to Pinyin, came to attention, and saluted.

She went out among them, smiling. Her guards all moved their umbrellas over her as she walked. "You're getting slow in your old age. You should have been here twenty minutes ago. Regardless, our job is to guard this ship, and the ambassador when she needs to go elsewhere. Set it up."

The guards split to surround the *Revenge*. Three started setting out equipment, whether motion sensors or something else, I couldn't say.

When Pinyin returned to the ramp, one of the older guards, with a shaved head, came up to Pinyin, folding their umbrella as they did. That's when I noticed their rather large backpack.

Pinyin turned to me. "This is my captain, Tanaka. When I am not around, they will help you. Tanaka, this is Deuce."

I shook Tanaka's hand and the three of us went inside, with me using my bracer to close the ramp.

Pinyin scampered up the ladder to summon Mikka back down. Soon we all gathered around the table.

Tanaka set the big backpack on the red tablecloth. "Sorry we were late. It took a little to gather what you asked.

Pinyin gestured to the backpack and nodded for Tanaka to open it. "I've been thinking about the black box. We may want to leave it here while we *appear* to take it elsewhere."

Tanaka pulled out some struts and panels and built two boxes about the size of the black box. Some of the pieces seem quite heavy, too.

When he finished, Pinyin pointed to each. "Since they are most vulnerable while on the move, we take them out, with four person teams. They go different directions to two different museums and the boxes stay in packs so no one can see. The museums put them in their vaults. Lastly, we hide the real one here somewhere."

I hadn't thought about that. "I can put it between the inner and outer hulls. Anyone familiar with ships would never think of that as a place you can even get to."

Pinyin gestured all around at the *Revenge*. "Then we just have to protect the ship." She looked at me. "Why do they want this ship anyway?"

I grinned and shrugged. "It's special. Let's call it faster than anything this size."

Pinyin cocked her head. "Then I suggest we make it into a honeypot."

13
HONEYPOT

Four days later, I tossed and turned in my bunk on the
Revenge, feeling useless and alone.

The day after the Mao debacle, Mikka had been
summoned to the Council of Planets man-made island out on
the bay east of Beijing. Pinyin, along with four other guards,
had gone with her, leaving me alone on *Hiram's Revenge* while
the Council heard testimony and debated.

I had prowled the decks, checked the food supplies, the
telemetry and status on everything, done routine
maintenance, and checked the repairs. Four or five times
each. I watched movies, but everything in my library seemed
old and familiar. I didn't dare connect to any outside network
for entertainment.

It wasn't like being alone on the *Revenge* was new to me. I
did it all the time, but usually I was lightyears from any other
humans rather than having a billion of them nearby.
Somehow, after being with Mikka for not even two months,
her absence left a glaring void.

Moreover, that void echoed my life back on Angel's Planet.
It made my lack of friends stand out. Earl might have been a
friend if he had a personality. Ramon was little more than an
acquaintance. Marta was nice, but a business associate. The
other pilots were barely that, even Winsome, though she
might be a friend if we ever spent much time together.

So, I paced from the bridge to the common room, with a
stop in the galley for a snack. Then I folded the gym out of the

ceiling and worked out. After that, another snack and attempting to read a book. Bored, I went down and circled the cargo hold. Mikka had returned the table to the event organizer, so even that space seemed echoing and empty.

Each night with Mikka gone, I laid in bed, fretting and lonely.

Today, though, as the sun set, Mikka had come back. Pinyin delivered her to the ramp, which I let down, then Pinyin departed for other business.

I hugged Mikka and walked her in. "How was it?"

She rolled her eyes. "Exhausting! They spent hours questioning me. Then hours questioning the Romans. Par representatives, notably Thurman, let me feed them questions for the Romans. Overall, there were belligerent questions, repetitive questions, absurdly long-winded questions. Bah!" She dismissed it all with a wave.

Chuckling, I headed to the ladder and up to the living deck. "Let's make empanadas for old-time sake."

"Cooking sounds wonderful."

Up we went. Then we cooked and chatted, just mundane stuff.

When we hit a pause, I leaned against the galley counter. I wanted to get out of here. I wanted to fly. I wanted a friend, or a lot of friends. "What's next?"

Mikka snorted. "Much debate. Then vote. I am uncertain. I have felt resistance, doubt, in some of the questions, but not from who." She leaned over to look at the batter as it mixed. "What about here? Anything happening?"

"Nothing at all." My voice sounded bitter.

Mikka ran a finger over the edge of the bowl and licked it. "That bad?"

I paced two steps into the hall and back. "I've been alone for years. Now it bothers me, gives me time to think that I'm not a real person."

Mikka started making coffee but didn't look at me. "You're a real person, this I kende. Why would you think this?"

I threw my hands at the sky, or really at space, and paced into the corridor. "My twin sister, she casts a long shadow, and all I do seems to be *just* like her."

From that, Mikka could figure out who I was.

Mikka picked up her cup and sipped her coffee. "A twin? Ah." She nodded to herself. "This we kende, um, understand, too. Ask yourself how you are like her and how different. Then whether the parts where you are like her are things you enjoy."

She had a point, but I wasn't sure I was ready to hear it yet. I folded my arms and pouted. "Why am I so alone when you aren't here?"

She lifted her cup toward her room. "You've had other passengers?"

I leaned against the corridor wall across from the galley. "Sure."

Mikka set down the cup, stepped in front of me, and took my hands. "But you were not venner with any of them?"

I snorted. "Friends? No. Most I could barely tolerate."

Mikka laughed and went back to cooking. "I apologize for befriending you."

I laughed so hard that I ended up on the floor.

That's when Pinyin returned, of course. "Are you two planning an orgy without me?"

Mikka smiled and waved a spoon. "No. Deuce was just evaluating my flight plans for a CPN expedition back to Eksil."

When the empanadas were finished baking, we went to the common room and shared them. Pinyin had never eaten the like, but she didn't mind the spice, and we had a good conversation. We reviewed our security plans and discussed what the Council of Planets might do.

Later, lying in bed not sleeping, I stared at the ceiling wondering if I could go back to my life on Angel's Planet. And if the bastards who created me would let me be if I didn't. Did they know I was the one who flew Mikka here?

Moreover, did I enjoy flying like my sister, or at least half as much as her?

I heard a thump. A moment later a light appeared on my bracer. A chill went through me as I picked it up off the nightstand. Someone had landed on the roof then opened the outer airlock door in the common room. First, I hit the button to lock my door and Mikka's. Then I pressed the panic button, which would radio Pinyin, who'd rigged a hammock in the cargo hold, and Tanaka. Tanaka would get the Lavender Shield people away from the ship as well as notifying the Beijing police and the Americas Secret Service.

Next, I donned my pressure suit, the bracer, and my flight helmet, plugging the helmet into a wall jack in my tiny quarters. Mikka and Pinyin would be getting into pressure suits, too, in case the intruders drained the air from the ship.

On my helmet, I brought up the internal security cameras and watched two men walk down the corridor to the bridge. They stopped to try both Mikka's door and mine, but didn't seem worried they couldn't get in. They went on to the bridge and climbed into the pilot and copilot seats.

Anger flared in me. They had no right to sit in Hiram's seat! Mikka I made an exception for. Not these intruders.

I locked the bridge door so they couldn't get out, then made sure the pressure was equalized between the bridge and the rest of the ship.

I radioed Beijing space port control. "Mayday. This is *SS Shadow Wing*. Intruders have boarded our ship. They are attempting to kidnap ambassador Retts."

I didn't get an answer, so I repeated the message. I still got no answer. Very strange

Now, we would wait. I needed them to know they couldn't fly the ship. Then it would be time for talking. Just to see, I swiped the security camera view of the bridge up onto the wall.

The man in the pilot's seat was trying to activate the gravity drive. The other guy didn't even have a flight helmet on. I couldn't hear anything, but they seemed to be talking to each other. The pilot looked frustrated.

At last, he stopped doing anything, so I opened the intercom. "You aren't going anywhere. You should probably give up now."

They ignored me. The copilot pulled out a computer and plugged it into my ship.

What the hell was he trying to do?

I shut off the intercom, brought up a virtual keyboard and looked at the drive control systems. It didn't take me long to find code changing. He was trying to hack past my block on starting the drives!

I'd put security on the controls, not the code. I didn't think they could get to the code. The drives should only start with my voice print and the bracer being present on the bridge. This guy was going to get past my locks.

I opened a private channel to Pinyin. "The honeypot is about to be broken. They'll be able to take off soon."

She paused before answering but sounded determined. "I will come up as soon as I can."

I just hoped she could deal with high-g maneuvers.

Wanting to hack-back against this guy in Hiram's seat, I wondered. If the copilot detected my presence in the system, that would be bad. He could probably lock me out. Still, at this point they wouldn't know how to operate my tri-modulated field. That would take hours of searching. I wondered if I could fool the pilot about the direction they were headed. If I froze or slowed the image in Lu-space, I might be able to turn the ship without them knowing, in Lu space, but not outside it, at least not anywhere near a planet.

I started setting it up.

A light tap on my door told me Pinyin had made it up to the corridor. If she got to the bridge before...

The drives started. The *Revenge* shot into the air at one g. Too fast. That would shatter the paving stones. And I'd landed so gently.

I opened a channel to Beijing control again. "Mayday! We're being kidnapped. They've taken over our ship. The ambassador is on board."

Still no reply. Something was very wrong.

Now I just had to hope the CPN wouldn't blow us up. And the invaders wouldn't notice my hacking. And that they didn't try to suck the air out of the rest of the ship, which they could only do if they noticed I'd equalized the bridge.

I hated this. Hated waiting. Hated not being in control of my ship.

I brought the outside view up on a different wall. The *Revenge* accelerated through the high clouds, shaking in the bumpy air, then we cleared all but the wispy high clouds. Radar showed CPN vessels closing in from above.

How much time did I have? How much did the pilot know? I'd jumped inside an atmosphere. He might try. I disabled the Lu-Space altitude display. Then I took a gravity scan up ahead, filtering out everything closer than a hundred-thousand klicks. Once in Lu space, maybe the pilot wouldn't pay attention.

Overhead, the navy ships closed in. We rose past fifty thousand meters. If he was going to jump, it would be soon. I had my finger on the trigger to change the Virtual Vision for him.

"What can I do to hjælp?" Mikka asked.

I jumped almost out of my skin.

Oh! They would almost *expect* an ambassador to try to talk them out of it. "Distract them! Make them pay attention to you!"

After laughing, Mikka switched the intercom and started talking.

The navy ships got within a thousand klicks. The pilot's finger reached for the jump button. He pressed it. The blue sky stretched and faded to the normal amorphous colors. I replaced the gravity scan with my movie. As an afterthought, I turned off the boost light.

"Tri-modulate. Decrease vertical vector one g. Turn ninety degrees right."

Mikka yelled at them to land or there would be serious consequences.

The pilot didn't seem to notice my course change. The *Revenge* obeyed me. "Turn ninety degrees right."

The *Revenge* dropped out of Lu space, headed back toward earth.

I unlocked the bridge door. "Pinyin, now!"

The pilot swore and took the joysticks to turn around again.

On the surveillance camera, Pinyin charged in. She yanked the pilot's Virtual Vision cable out. Then she grabbed the copilot's computer and smashed it into the wall. The pilot tried to unbuckle. Pinyin kicked him in the head. With her steel-toed boots. The helmet cracked.

The copilot launched himself at her. She ducked and flipped him. He landed against the bulkhead, feet in the air. Pinyin shot him with a stun gun.

My ship was mine again. I took a long breath and flipped open the orbital control channel. "This is the *SS Shadow Wing*. We have regained control of the ship, and request landing clearance for Beijing Spaceport."

Someone from orbital control finally answered. "*Shadow Wing*, please proceed to Armstrong Station."

I didn't like how that sounded. I unstrapped from my bunk and dashed for the bridge. "Mikka, stay there. Pinyin, get those two secured and strap in."

Ignoring me, Mikka dashed out of her room to help lift the groggy man out of the pilot's seat. As soon as he was clear, I slipped in. I buckled up and jacked in, going through the motions without thought.

The pilot's seat smelled like a man, a strange man. I wanted to scrub the whole thing. He'd invaded my refuge!

I checked the location of the CPN ships in the area.

We were surrounded. Six destroyers closed on our position. They should have just let us land.

I shook my head. "Something is very wrong here. I'm going to play along."

Pinyin and Mikka dragged the two hijackers back to the common room. A light on my heads-up display said they'd deployed the gym. The equipment had things you could tie people to.

Next, I contacted orbital control. "Roger, Armstrong. Heading your way. We've captured the men who tried to steal our ship."

Again, I got no reply, so I tried a third time.

I wondered if they recorded my broadcasts. If so, I had to try again. "Armstrong station, this is a diplomatic mission. The only acceptable landing place is Beijing Space Port. We just survived an assassination attempt. Please respond."

They didn't answer. As if I hadn't even spoken.

With a sigh, I turned the *Revenge's* roof toward Armstrong and accelerated toward the station at a sedate one g. The destroyers escorted me in, so I restored my special features to the heads up displays. I had a boost. Would it be enough?

Mikka, back in her room, interrupted. "Would your employers know what's going on?

They might. We didn't know anyone else who would.

Pinyin piped up. "All secure back here. Contact Tanaka. He'll know something."

First, I opened a tight beam to the Lavender Shield headquarters. "This is Deuce for Tanaka. What's going on down there?"

Fortunately, we had twenty more minutes to get to Armstrong, so I homed in on the Denver network beacon. From there, I entered the code they'd given me.

For the first time in forever, I got an answer. "Hello. This Americas Regional Government. How can I help you?"

Relief flooded through me. Someone who would talk to me! "Hello, this is Deuce, pilot for Ambassador Retts. We need some assistance."

"Thank you, please hold."

Some benign music came on, which I found annoying. It didn't last long, though.

A male voice said. "Hello, Deuce. This is Captain Burns, America's Secret Service. What the hell is going on over there?"

He was supposed to tell *me*, damn it. At least he was talking to me. "We were hijacked but have regained control of the ship. We're being directed to Armstrong Station. I'd rather not go there. No one is talking to me. What is going on?"

After a long pause, Captain Burns sighed. "I do not know. Word here is that Ambassador Retts attempted to flee and was stopped. Hmm. There is one other thing. That Mao character does not seem to have been suborned. His manager ordered him to destroy the device. I don't like this. I'll get back to you."

I imagined him reaching to cut me off.

I smacked the food cooler beside my seat. "Wait! I'm going to try for my original landing spot at that ranch in the mountains near Denver. Can you make sure I don't get shot down?"

Captain Burns paused. "I will do what I can. Can you give me an hour?"

I snorted "If I survive the next ten minutes, I can give you an hour, two if you need it."

"Roger that. See you soon."

He cut the connection, and I wondered if he intended to meet us at the ranch. Then the other thing caught my attention; Mao's *boss* had told him to destroy the black box. Damn.

Pieces began to fall in place and my gut began tying itself in knots. Beijing spaceport and Armstrong station were not answering me. No one acknowledged the hijacking. But Captain Burns talked to me. The Asia bloc dominated the Earth government, and controlled Beijing police and the space port there.

Pinyon broke my train of thought. "Has Tanaka replied? Has anyone replied?"

Double damn. "No. And the Asia Bloc is one of the few groups who could arrest or suppress the Lavender Shield. I'm not a spy, but if I'm right, we're in trouble."

"Do you have a plan?" Mikka said.

"Not a good one. We'll have to trust the people who hired me. Hold on."

Before I did anything, I checked on our destroyer escort. They still surrounded us; except they were staying away from my path toward Armstrong. That would be my escape route. They'd love that.

I opened a channel to Armstrong again. "Armstrong, this is *Shadow Wing*. Beginning my deceleration."

With slow deliberation, I flipped the *Revenge*. They were expecting me to put the bottom toward Armstrong. I stopped with the bridge facing the station instead.

"Boost!" I slammed the thrust pedal to the floor.

Hiram's Revenge leapt forward at just over 5 gs. Straight toward Armstrong.

It took seconds for anyone to react. I dropped chaff to deflect laser cannons.

I opened a broadcast channel on every frequency I could. "Mikka, say something."

"This is Ambassador Retts. We have been hijacked and are now being obstructed in our attempt to return to Beijing. As such, we refuse orders to dock at Armstrong station. I will provide details later."

Two of the six destroyers fired two missiles each. One fired a laser barrage. Armstrong station yelled over the radio that they would fire at us.

I shifted my course so we would pass Armstrong outside its orbit.

The green light came on. I hit the jump button.

14
A Light in the Darkness

The missiles closing in from the sides vanished as the stars stretched and faded. Earth, Armstrong station, and the six destroyers all stretched and faded, too. I took a breath, relaxing just a little.

The effort it took to breathe reminded me. I dropped us back to a more sedate 3 gs, which gave me another boost. I also turned thirty degrees to the right. That way a light plume would not be in the direction they'd seen the *Revenge* jump. It would slow down any response.

I took us thirty light-minutes out and fell back to normal space. Flipping the Revenge, I powered us to 3 gs, heading back toward Earth, flying top first so gravity was toward the deck.

Then I took my helmet off and flipped open the intercom. "Mikka, Pinyin, we need to talk."

When we'd all gathered on the bridge, I rose to face them. "I think the resistance Mikka felt during the questioning was the Asia Bloc. Now, if I'm right, they've conspired with the Romans against us."

Pinyin started to say something, stopped, and at last looked up at the stars overhead. "Oh. I should have seen. Damn. The Asia Bloc has a *huge,* vested interest in the status quo." She pointed at the ambassador. "Mikka here is likely to upset that status quo. And you're right, they are one of a small set of groups that could keep my people from answering."

Mikka folded her arms and leaned against the door jamb. "What do we do? How do we counter them?"

Every option had serious risks, but I ticked them off on my fingers. "We really only have two choices that I see. Pinyin can correct me. We either attempt to go down to North America as originally scheduled and hope the America Bloc can protect us and get word out. Or we give up and leave."

Pinyin cocked her head, thinking a moment. "I'm not seeing anything else. I do have friends back in Beijing. I might be able to get information, but they won't be able to take on the Asia Pac."

A third hot, impossible landing awaited us. Everyone was going to know about my ship.

Mikka frowned. "Will there be press there when we get down?"

Having them there, like in the Forbidden City, would be huge. "The question is whether to trust the Americas Bloc to do it or invite them ourselves?"

Mikka rolled her eyes. "At this point, trust no one. Invite them."

That reminded me of something else. I turned to our security consultant. "Pinyin, do you know any reputable security firms in the Denver area or Western Colorado? I think you could use a subcontractor."

She rubbed her chin. "I will find someone. Might be tricky from this far out."

An hour later, after several queries to satellite relays, we had only basic info, although we had notified the press. Pinyin had cooked us some tasty dumplings, though.

With all of us frustrated by the one-hour round trip communication time to Earth, I sat down in the pilot's chair and jacked in. Before changing course, I changed my responder back to *Hiram's Revenge*, wishing I had a third option. I couldn't use *Shadow Wing* on this approach since I was just getting us closer.

At last, I accelerated toward Earth again, keeping it to a sedate three gs. The jump light came on, and I pressed the button. The stars faded and I turned the *Revenge* twice in Lu space to make the approach I wanted.

We fell out beyond the moon's orbit, a hundred degrees from the direction we'd taken when leaving. It was a standard, if long, approach for a two-g ship. As soon as the stars appeared, I radioed Armstrong station for a berth, saying I was bringing new computer games from Tanterra and a marketing specialist to boot.

I flipped the *Revenge* over bottom-first and decelerated at two gs.

Twenty minutes later, Armstrong gave us a berthing assignment. By then, Pinyin had located a security company and hired six guards for the next two days, with an option for a week.

Next, I made sure Mikka, sitting in Hiram's seat, was on the line when I called Captain Burns again. "Hello, Captain. This is Deuce. We should be down in less than an hour."

"Good. We're almost ready. You'll have to bypass orbital control. We can't get to them."

"Hello, Captain. This is Ambassador Retts. We have called the media people. Please let them into the landing area when they arrive."

The captain paused a moment. "Um, we do have our own reporters we work with."

"Good! Invite them, too! The more people who know about what has happened the better. See you soon. Oh, and when my security detail arrives, make sure they are waiting when we land."

Mikka broke the connection. She tapped the console. "It's going to be a circus."

It was time to implement the rest of the plan. I called Armstrong again. "Um, sorry to bother you, Armstrong, but my passenger has never been here to Sol system. He wants to take a cruise around to see the sites. We'll be back in about eight hours, I expect. Keep the seat warm for us."

Orbital control laughed. "Roger, *Hiram's Revenge*. We get this sort of thing more often than you might think. Catch you on the inbound."

I adjusted our heading toward Jupiter, left of the sun on the far side, and accelerated again, still at two gs. After a suitable time, I hit the jump button.

Once more the stars faded to amorphous colors. I turned, heading toward the sun. Once I was between the Earth and sun, I fell out again. The sun would hide my light plume.

I turned us toward Earth. Mikka and I got up to change clothes again, back into our official Eksil uniforms, such as they were. We planned to make another spectacular entrance.

Back in the cockpit, I jacked in and took a deep breath. One more ridiculous dive through the atmosphere. One more ridiculous landing.

Mikka patted my arm. "You can do this. I trust you."

I gave her shoulder a shove. "It's just that I'm supposed to be hiding."

I punched the Revenge to three gs and flat-shifted, so we flew bridge forward. I'd entered the flight plan into the computer already, an even closer approach than before. I switched the responder back to *Shadow Wing*.

The green jump light came on.

"Execute!"

We bugged out, rising into Lu space, and then descending again.

The *Revenge* fell out in the stratosphere, engines still online. A thunderclap echoed out from the ship. I accelerated downward, leaving a trail of smoke and steam as we came in west to east over the desert.

Armstrong station and the CPN both shouted at me to heave to and surrender. Fighters launched from California and Texas. Two destroyers headed down from above.

Mikka got on the radio and let them all know she was an ambassador with diplomatic immunity.

I started decelerating as we screamed down through the atmosphere, figuring those fighters were too far away to catch me now. I extended the *Revenge's* control surfaces, adjusting our flight toward that ranch near the Gunnison River.

Then I got a collision alert. In space those happened at hundreds of kilometers. When I looked, the squadron of fighters from California was closing fast. They left condensation trails too, which gravity drives wouldn't do, but the fighters did show up on the gravity scan.

I still had a boost to stop us. I tipped the nose down and boosted. I needed to get to the ground before the fighters arrived.

The fighters closed. A red light appeared in my heads up display; a target lock.

The radio crackled. "This is Interceptor Squadron Charlie. *Shadow Wing*, cease your descent."

I smacked the food box again. "Damn."

I pulled the nose up to level and reduced deceleration to two gs.

Three fighters circled around in front of me. They had rockets in addition to gravity drives! That's how they'd caught me so fast.

The radio came on again. "This is Lieutenant Commander Ravenry. *Shadow Wing*, what are your intentions?"

At least he hadn't shot me down. That boded well. I flipped the mic to reply. "This Captain Deuce. Our primary intention is to land at a ranch here." I sent him the coordinates.

"What weapons are you carrying?"

That brought an ironic grin to my lips. "The *Shadow Wing* has no weapons at present. You can check my laser turret yourself. I will open my missile bays as well. Stay calm."

I punched up the maintenance menus and found the one to load missiles. It complained that the gravity drives were still on, so I overrode the security protocol. The hatches, one on each side above the cargo bay, opened. No missiles waited inside.

Other fighters circled me, checking my weapon status.

The commander spoke again. "Captain Deuce, we concur that you have no weapons. Gutsy given we still get shark attacks sometimes." He paused. "We've gotten conflicting orders regarding you. One set said you're a terrorist planning to bomb something. The other said to let you pass."

I almost laughed, but my stomach was still tied in knots. These interceptors could blow the *Revenge* out of the sky without a thought. I raised one hand, as if they could see. "I vote for letting us pass."

"We will escort you down, but we will need to inspect your cargo holds and the like for bombs or other weapons."

Mikka stirred in her seat. "Could this be a ruse to get on board?"

I doubted these pilots were dishonest but protecting ourselves would take a little finesse.

I rubbed my palm on my pants. "Roger, Commander. At the sufferance of Ambassador Retts, we will allow one or two people onboard. This *is* a diplomatic ship."

It took a little for him to respond, perhaps checking with his commanding officer. "Two people will be acceptable. Proceed with your flight plan."

"Roger and thank you."

"The CPN does not like to be manipulated, Captain."

I shut off the radio and cruised down through the atmosphere. Since I was descending slower than planned, I took a circle route down through wispy clouds. Two valleys spread below, with one river coming from the east, the other from the southeast. The ranch was a dozen kilometers south of where the two waterways met, still in the broad river valley.

We came in from east to west over a large mesa with pine trees on the lower slopes. Then out over the valley, where scrub brush seemed to rule. On the far side, where the land rose again into higher peaks, grav-cars circled.

The coordinates I was given were there. White fences, that didn't look like they could really keep people out, surrounded a large pasture. Where the ground started to rise again on the far slope stood a large, old house, perhaps older than the colony on Thurman. It was two stories with a wooden porch and steep gabled roof that held solar panels and wind generators, and white stucco walls with arched window openings.

Out in the pasture, a square had been marked off, with people waiting outside the perimeter. The square was large enough to land a starship.

I flew the *Revenge* over to the square and stopped a hundred meters off the ground. Then I descended, dead slow, straight down. Most of our fighter escort hovered overhead, but two descended with me, much closer than I normally wanted another ship.

As soon as we touched down, Mikka and I scrambled from our seats. We dashed back to the common room, where

Pinyin was preparing to usher the prisoners down into the cargo hold.

She gestured at my sidearm. "Guard them from below, please."

I drew my plasma pistol and went down the ladder first, standing well back. "Come on down, boys."

When the grumpy prisoners descended, they glared at me and rubbed their hands. I directed them to the top of the ramp and had them sit.

Pinyin came down and secured them again with a device on their legs and handcuffs like the ones I'd been in on New Zion after my graduation flight. Then she came to attention behind them and nodded at me.

Mikka came down, and the two of us stepped onto the ramp, almost at the bottom. I used my bracer to start the ramp down.

We made our entrance the same as we did in the Forbidden City. At the bottom of the ramp, facing outward, stood four men and two women dressed in purple shirts and black pants. Beyond them stood what looked like secret service and government personnel, inside the white fence. Craning necks and lifting cameras high, two dozen people waited behind the fence. Over by the house people were setting out a buffet.

Mikka raised her hands, and spoke, voice amplified by the *Revenge*. "I am Ambassador Mikka Retts from Eksil. My staff and I have just thwarted an attempted hijacking, possibly two. Someone did not want us here talking to you. We will need to do some investigating, but we want to include you. Please broadcast everything far and wide. Publicity will help uncover what is happening."

At that point a man and a woman in flight suits walked around from the *Revenge's* flank, coming face to face with our temporary security force.

Mikka glanced at them and continued. "First, we have to convince these good pilots that we mean no harm to anyone." She inclined her head toward the pilots. "Lieutenant Commander Ravenry? As agreed, please come aboard. And search for weapons. The only ones are sidearms that belong to my pilot and head of security."

The purple guards parted to let the pilots through. One of them followed the pilots up.

I extended a hand to Lieutenant Commander Ravenry. "I'm Deuce."

He shook my hand. "Ravenry. Shall we?"

I started up the ramp, "Of course. It's rather boring." When we reached the top, I pointed a thumb at the prisoners. "Those are the hijackers, the physical rather than political ones."

Ravenry gave me a hooded glance. Then he stopped in the cargo bay and chuckled. "That would be empty."

The other pilot pulled out a sensor device of some kind and swept it around. After a moment, she shook her head. "It's clean."

"May we go up?" Ravenry asked, pointing at the ladder.

Reluctant, I still nodded. "Of course."

I led them up and showed them the rather boring personnel deck, first the common room, then the cabins, head, and galley. Last, we made it to the bridge. I stepped in.

Ravenry shook his head as he craned his neck to look side to side. "Looks boring, but it doesn't fly boring. What did you do to this thing?"

I leaned with one arm against the bridge's side wall and grinned. "I made a modification or two."

"Ha!" He cuffed my elbow. "I've been watching film of your flight into Beijing. That wasn't just a modification. It's why they finally let us fly the rocket-assist ships."

I looked over my shoulder at them sitting so nice and still on the grass. "Those things are fast."

"For short periods only." He glanced in at the bridge. "So ordinary. Oh, well. Someone will figure it out."

I hadn't thought of that. I should have. It was a fundamental principle of engineering; if you know it can be done, you can recreate it with time.

I frowned. "That would be true. I'll have to see what I can do about that."

The other pilot, having snooped around with her device, even to the point of going through all the furniture in the common room, shrugged. "All clear, Commander."

He gave me a wry grin. "I did want to see and meet you. We'll be leaving a couple fighters overhead, but as much to protect you as anything else."

We headed back down to the cargo deck. "Given what's been happening, I would appreciate the protection."

When Ravenry and his pilot departed, I found Pinyin displaying the prisoners to the press and America's Bloc Secret Service.

Mikka raised her hand toward the prisoners, still speaking so everyone could hear. "Captain Burns, I believe you will find these two to be spies from Nova Roma. The question is who was helping them?"

The short man in front of her, who had an immaculate suit and a long ponytail decorated with colorful beads, put hands on hips and glared at the duo. "I will endeavor to discover just that."

Burns signaled to two women, also in immaculate suits, who presented themselves to the purple guards. Pinyin nodded, and the purples let the women through to escort the prisoners away.

I stepped down beside Pinyin, who was near the bottom of the ramp now. "Purple?"

She grimaced. "It was the best they could do on short notice. They do seem tolerably competent, though."

I chuckled, appreciating her high standards.

At that, Mikka turned to me. "Captain, we will need bridge video and anything else you can put together."

"Of course, Ambassador." And I would make sure to edit out anything about the Revenge's special abilities.

I walked back up the ramp to the engineering station, feeling useless again, but also having a great deal to think about. After the hours working with Pinyin and Mikka during and after the hijacking, I now felt alone again. I wanted to find a home and find myself. I'd escaped the bastards who created me. What would they do to get me back?

Perhaps they'd just tried.

That made me want to put missiles in those empty bays and go blow something up. But, fleetingly, I had the best ship in this part of space. I needed to leverage that, but how?

I was going to need a lawyer, and I only knew one. Before I could think of why not, I got online, using a secure virtual computer, and sent a courier to New Zion summoning Abraham Stone to Thurman. He'd been the man trying to get me charged and tried while the bastards tried to drop the charges after my Solomon Tech graduation stunt. The bastards had won that round, but I'd expected them to.

I ran through the video one more time to make sure I hadn't shown anything to reveal the *Revenge's* capabilities. After that, I walked back down the ramp. Then, when Mikka was ready, flipped the video, which included all my calls to Beijing space port and Armstrong Station.

The reporters were impressed, but I could tell the smartest ones zeroed in on the lack of answers from anyone to my repeated queries.

And that was all the work for the day. We spent hours showing the video over and over and eating a buffet with government officials and reporters. I ended up near Mikka and Pinyin at a table up on the porch for all to see.

That night, exhausted beyond words and still having fighter cover overhead, Mikka, Pinyin, and I went to sleep on board *Hiram's Revenge.*

In the morning, too early, Pinyin woke us. "Something's happening. Can we get the news on?"

First, we opted to cook waffles, which Pinyin found amusing. At last, we ended up in the common room, and I projected from a secure computer to the far wall above the ladder.

Then we all watched and listened, even switching to new feeds on occasion. The reporters had traced the lack of response from Beijing Control and Armstrong Station to specific controllers and found other sources to corroborate that I had sent at least one message that didn't get answered.

Now evening in China, at least one of the controllers had been fired, which was a mistake. She talked to reporters detailing how she was *ordered* not to answer any calls from the *Shadow Wing.*

The reporters were trying to work their way up the chain of command, with lots and lots of speculation included. How high will it go? Who ordered this despicable behavior?

Then Captain Burns called. His call had video, so I put him up in place of the news. He looked quite pleased with himself. "Hello, Ambassador. I assume you're watching the news, but I wanted to give you a bit of an inside scoop. The internal investigations have gotten much higher than the controller's immediate bosses. We're already hearing talk about a no-confidence vote for President Adhikari. The walls will come tumbling down, I think."

President Adhikari? He was head of the Council of Planets, though he came from Asia Pac. All the presidents of the council had. That was how much Earth dominated it. Would that change now?

Mikka stood. "Will they grant my embassy?"

Burns pursed his lips. "Nothing is certain yet, but I think either that or a CPN mission to Eksil. One or the other, perhaps both. Whoever was behind this whole thing tried to say you ran away to avoid people finding out you were a fraud. You rather disproved the running away, and thus the fraud, too."

Mikka inclined her head. "Thank you, Captain. We will be out shortly. This time I think the reporters will have stories to tell *me.*"

Burns laughed and broke the connection.

That night, I sat down at the little table on the *Revenge* with Mikka and Pinyin to eat some flatbread with beans and mutton that Captain Burns had procured. While we basked in our victory and I tried to swallow the strange flavors, Mikka spoke of her hope for the vote.

At last, she turned to me. "Well, Deuce, have you decided whether to maintain your exile or not?

I could stay here, with Mikka, where I was useless, but had a friend, or go back to Angel's Planet where I had uses, but no friends. My third option seemed better, given the fleeting value of engineering breakthroughs. "I'm going home to Thurman to sell the changes I've made to my ship."

That was something my sister had never done.

15
HOME AGAIN

Two weeks later, I fell out in the Tau Ceti system, feeling anticipation and fear. I floated system-inward out near the orbit of the gas giant Cassandra, but nowhere near the planet, hence nowhere near another ship. I let the gravity scans and system traffic buoys fill me in on what ships were around.

The bastards who'd created me would know I was at Earth. I doubted they missed who had brought Mikka. They would know I came here, too. What would they do, though? They couldn't make me join the CPN. They couldn't make me work for Pauley Spaceways again. They could hire me for dangerous jobs. Maybe they already had, and I'd been desperate enough to take it.

I could always leave, except I'd hired two couriers, one to fetch Earl and one to fetch my lawyer, Abraham Stone, from New Zion. I'd even gotten the Americas Bloc to pay for the couriers as part of my expenses.

My employers had been quite pleased when the Asia Bloc lost its hold on most of Earth politics in the scandal. The new Council of Planets president was from Thurman, and under her direction had approved a temporary embassy for Mikka and a CPN expedition to Eksil. I suspected the Americas thought adding a planet to the council would accomplish what Mikka and I had done in a couple of weeks. It needed to be done, though. It was time for the frontier planets to get a voice.

I opened a channel to the nearest communication relay and sent a message to retired Admiral Cinti Arias, who had bought *Hiram's Revenge* for me with Brandy's inheritance. "Have the roof open tomorrow. I'm coming home."

An hour and a half later, the response came in. "Roger that. Look forward to seeing you."

Fourteen hours later, I accelerated inward, but at just half a g. I wanted to perform a delicate maneuver. I flat-shifted, so I was flying bridge-forward. Then I plotted a course to the admiral's house, such that I would fall out with little velocity inside the atmosphere.

Before jumping, I checked the weather. Sure enough, there was a thunderstorm a few dozen kilometers away. I anticipated where the storm would be when I got there, adjusted my course, and hit the jump button.

The stars faded into Lu-space colors. Less than a minute later, the colors stretched and brightened. Then the volume of my Lu-space bubble pushed the storm outward. The vacuum let it crash back in. The *Revenge* shook from the impact. Thunder rolled outside. Wind buffeted my ship.

I laughed as my body flew against the restraints. I dropped down, looking for smoother air. My altitude fell below two thousand meters with zero visibility. At eight hundred, I emerged beneath the clouds into the rain. I'd come in west to east, but today, clouds obscured the mountains to the north.

Pauley City spread southeast of my flightpath on the right. It looked small and quaint compared to Beijing. It *was* small and quaint compared to Beijing. Launching City spaceport, farther away due south, was dwarfed by Beijing's spaceport, too.

As I crossed through the cold front, wind tossed *Hiram's Revenge.* Then the admiral's house appeared ahead. A large hangar, with the roof open, sat out back between the house and the stream. A new walkway led from the back patio down to a new deck by the stream. The country house, with its rounded edges, solar panels, and wind turbines on the roof, had even more flowers and trees than it had when I left. Its blue and gray color scheme seemed odd and familiar.

I brought *Hiram's Revenge* to a stop and hovered a kilometer away. I couldn't catch my breath. From this place

I'd made my escape, and now I was coming back. I still wanted to find those bastards and hit them over the head.

Forcing myself to take long, slow breaths, I calmed the panic and the fury. Then four people came out onto the back patio and looked up at the *Revenge*. Two of them had shaved heads. Joyce and Cinti had invited my parents over. Cinti was so thoughtful, or maybe it was Joyce. Very thoughtful, regardless.

My eyes stung as I flew on, stopping over the hangar. Then I descended, dead slow, down through the open roof, to where I had first seen *Hiram's Revenge*. I bumped down, a little harder than I intended, but my front strut was still jury-rigged.

I shut down the drives and sat there, letting the vibrations fade from my body. At last, I jacked out, unstrapped, and rose. I didn't hurry out the back airlock and down the ladder; I knew they would wait, and I wanted to savor the anticipation. It didn't matter what happened tomorrow. Today I would spend with my parents and my old friends.

Having *young* friends would have been nice, but Cinti and Joyce would do for now.

By the time I got down, the four of them stood by the hangar's side door, waiting. Jo and Jeffers surged forward, wrapping me in a family hug.

Jo spoke into my hair. "Burgundy, we're so glad to see you."

It felt good to have someone call me by my name. I squeezed them tighter.

Eventually, Jeffers pulled back a little. "We are guests here."

I kissed both their cheeks, then turned to Cinti and Joyce. "Thank you for having me and inviting my parents."

"Don't be silly," Joyce said as she stepped up to hug me.

Cinti hugged me next, then held me at arm's length. "That was you flying the new ambassador to Earth?"

I ducked my head a little. "That was me. Who told you?"

"Teddy did," Jeffers said, coming up behind.

"Teddy?"

Cinti laughed. "Jackson." Then she gave me a sidelong glance. "What I want to know is how you *did* all that?" Blinking, Cinti stopped and glanced up at the storm. She frowned. "That thunder. You just fell out inside the atmosphere, didn't you?"

"Well, I didn't want everyone to know I was here."

Cinti rolled her eyes and looked at my parents. "She didn't bother telling Memnon control that she was coming down. Or even here at all."

Joyce herded us all toward the deck by the river. "Come, come. I have food all ready for us."

When I glanced back at the approaching storm, Cinti laughed. I understood why when we stepped through a small gravity field as we walked onto the deck. It would push the rain away.

We ate and laughed and talked for hours inside our dry bubble in a thunderstorm. Then Joyce put us all up for the night.

The next morning, after a leisurely brunch and more conversation—I astonished Cinti by talking about flying with the door open—I rode back into the city with my parents. I let them off at the Baxter Building and went on alone to see the one friend my age that I could still drop in on: Kaia, my roommate at Solomon Tech.

On the way, I stopped to get Greek food for six, because I wasn't sure how many kids she had now, and a bottle of champagne. When she and I had travelled back from New Zion to Thurman together, in that big suite I'd made the bastards pay for, we'd had a lot of champaign. And the *Arcturus* had specialized in Greek food.

When I gave it the address, my car took me down into the tunnels where it joined a train of other cars. Together, we went across town until the train separated and my car took a ramp upward. It emerged at a group of apartment buildings that surrounded a park for kids. A school lay at the center of the park. The car rose to the third floor and docked.

When the door opened, I emerged into a corridor with tan tile flooring and blue walls. I walked down to apartment 377 and rang the bell.

Children's voices yelling filtered into the hall. They ran over, but apparently had to wait on mom. Phan Cadence Kaia opened the door looking harried. A strand of dark hair trailed across her face. The rest seemed matted, and her eyes drooped.

When she saw me, a bright smile bloomed on her face. "Burgundy! I haven't seen you in ages. Come in! Don't mind the mess. Is that food? Did you bring us food? How are you doing? *What* are you doing? Where have you been? Kids, this is my friend Burgundy." She indicated a girl about two and a boy about three or so. "Burgundy, this is Bian and Junior."

"Mom! I'm Andre now!"

"Sorry, Andre."

Kaia fairly dragged me inside, and took the bag from me, talking the entire time. I let the comforting words flow over me. I'd forgotten how I'd grown to love her ceaseless chatter.

Overcome with affection, nostalgia, something, maybe just all the friends I'd had at Solomon Tech, I hugged Kaia. "I missed you."

Kaia hugged me back, as if being in my arms was her only refuge from the storm.

Too soon she broke away to set the bag of food on the table. "Oh, that smells heavenly! Where have you been anyway?"

"Planeta De Angel. I'm a freelance pilot. I have my own ship and everything. In fact, the best ship in the galactic arm."

Kaia plopped into a chair and started getting the food out. "Angel's Planet? Is Julio there?"

Julio, one of our other friends, came from there, but I'd never found him. It would not have been so lonely with Julio around. "No. I don't think he went back."

Bian and Andre appeared as if by magic when Kaia opened the first box of food, the gyro meat. Andre wrinkled his nose. "What's that, Mommy? It smells funny."

"Lunch, Junior. Wash up. Get some plates."

Bian grabbed a small piece and stuck it in her mouth. Then she made a face and spit it out.

Kaia rolled her eyes and retrieved the meat from the floor. "Your life sounds exciting."

I helped her get the food out. "It can be. It's also lonely. That's part of why I'm back." The amount of food reminded me, so I looked around. "Where is Andre senior?"

Kaia scowled. "I kicked the bastard out."

They'd seemed so good together the one time I'd seen them. "Why? What happened."

"Cat happened."

Oh, dear. Another friend from college, Cat tended to seduce anyone and everyone. "Damn her. She should have known better."

Little Andre brought plates, and we dished up pitas, gyro meat, cucumber salad, falafels, olives, feta cheese, several sauces, and baklava. While Kaia and I dug in, the kids ate pitas and used falafels to try the various dips.

At last, the kids ran off, flinging baklava crumbs everywhere.

Kaia scowled at the mess and ran a hand through her hair. "I should have known better about Cat. How long are you staying?"

"A few months, at least. I hired the lawyer I used on New Zion to come help me negotiate with Pauley Spaceways, and I sent for my starship mechanic from Angel's Planet, because no one else touches *Hiram's Revenge*."

Kaia looked startled, then reached out to touch my hand. "You named your ship *Hiram's Revenge*? I always wondered why the two of you never got together. I mean, you were perfect for each other."

Sadness washed over me as I recalled my one tryst with Hiram in the grove among the woody ferns. And he'd understood that I had to go. He didn't even ask why. "Had to. Too many secrets, too many people plotting how my life would go."

"Who would do that? And why?"

Still unable to tell her the whole truth, I shrugged. "The people who paid for our suite on the Arcturus. But now I used my engineering skills, and maybe did what they wanted me to do anyway. Still, I'm going to be rich."

If I licensed the technology to Pauley Spaceways, and got a fee per ship, I'd have so much money the bastards wouldn't be able to do a thing to me. A different form of escape. And I'd used my engineering skills. Brandy didn't have those. It was a start. All me and not her, and not avoiding being her either.

Kaia shook her head. "Your life never made sense to me."

I wrapped a pita around some more meat and spooned on some tzatziki sauce. Then I waved the thing toward Launching City and the Pauley Spaceways offices. "You know, if this contract comes through, I'll tell you all of it." Because then I will have enough money that it wouldn't matter. "What have you been up to?"

She waved at the ground. "I just help maintain and upgrade the automatic car system here in Pauley City. They want to expand to some of the outlying areas now, too."

A shriek from the other room interrupted her.

Kaia rolled her eyes. "But mostly I raise those brats. Where are you staying?"

I frowned a little, then turned a hand up. "Probably with my parents. Admiral Arias would let me stay if I asked."

Kaia looked down, then glanced up at me, almost shy. "Would you like to stay here with me? I could use a roommate again."

I imagined the noise, and the mess, and meeting Kaia's friends from work. She had to have those. This was Kaia after all. I'd have to play with the kids a lot, but after they were in bed, Kaia and I would drink wine and I'd listen to her chatter about nothing and everything. My parents would be disappointed, but I hadn't lived with them for years. It would feel weird to go back now. Maybe this wouldn't be a long-term home, but my exile was over, and I'd started the journey to become my own person.

"I would be delighted to be your roommate again."

The End

See below for Chapter 1 of **Sisters' Homecoming**, Clark Family Legend, Book VI

Acknowledgements and Dedication

Please remember to leave a review for this book at your favorite retailer.

This book is dedicated to Walt Friesen, my uncle who will always make you think about your spirituality and your emotional wellbeing.

Visit my web site at:

http://www.richardfriesen.net

If you like my stories, consider becoming a patron to help me with the costs of editing and cover art. You also get early access to stories and inside information on what I'm doing:

https://www.patreon.com/richardfriesen

Like superhero stories? Answer this: how can falling asleep be a superpower? Narcolepsy's opponents, and friends, and anyone who happens by, find out quickly and regret it.

<u>Narcolepsy Falls Asleep</u>

<u>Narcolepsy is Shocked</u>

****

Look for my epic fantasy series, **The Dreaming King Saga** in your favorite online bookstore now. Remember: he who dreams of the kingdom is king.

<u>The Tower of Dreams</u>

<u>An Uncivil War</u>

<u>On Black Mesa</u>

<u>The Gates of Heaven</u>

****

These professionals did wonderful work on this book:

Editing: Mia Kleve

MRK'd Up Editing

****

Cover Art: GermanCreative at Fiverr.com

****

This is a work of fiction. Any resemblance to people real or imaginary is unintended.

Sisters' Homecoming
1
Change of Plans

Earth Colony: Angel's Planet
Thurman Colony Year 292
Burgundy Lee's Freelance Diary

The meandering spaceport on Planeta de Angel seemed strange now, after spending time in Beijing and Launching City where things had been built with a purpose and a plan. I stepped out the door of Earl's shop and stopped. There on the left, a row of windows looked out over the Precipice, a stunning view of a steaming lake bordered by sharp ridges that kept the lava flows out of the water and the roiling methane atmosphere. And yet, no one came out to see it. The only people to make it this far needed to talk to Earl, the best ship mechanic on the planet, about something wrong on their starship.

With a snort of amusement at the idea of being the first "tourist" in this corridor, I strode inward toward the main terminal, turning left, then right, and right again. I passed airlock doors leading to docking berths. I'd had one of those once, could have again, but I wasn't staying long, and Earl, my starship mechanic and maybe friend, was fine parking my ship, the now famous and unique *Hiram's Revenge* in his shop. Form the outside it looked like an ordinary small freighter with a hatch on the rear of the personnel deck on top and a ramp up to the cargo bay, and painted black of course, with not markings. It looked like an ordinary freighter from the inside too, but it wasn't.

This trip into the domed town of Puerto Fronterizo, I intended to see some old friends, so I'd strapped my plasma pistol on for the first time in over a year.

I'd left from here to go pick up Ambassador Retts on Eksil and take her to Earth, which resulted in showing off how *Hiram's Revenge* could maneuver in Lu Space, which no other ship could do, yet. Our little adventure had gotten Eksil added to the Council of Planets and brought down the president of said council, when it came out that he'd conspired to stop us.

The only reason I'd come back was that Earl had wanted to come home. While on Thurman after leaving Ambassador Retts on Earth, Earl and I, along with my lawyer, Abraham Stone, had negotiated a lucrative contract with Pauley Spaceways. Both of us were set for life. Together we'd changed the way hyper-jumps in Lu space could be done, and in addition to a few hundred million up front we would get half a percent of each ship sold with our modifications. Flying Earl back here myself seemed like the least I could do.

When the familiar spaceport scents of hydraulic oil and warm electronics, plus the whine of gravity drives and the hubbub of people coming and going reached my senses, a smile broke on my face. I was a freelance pilot, and this was familiar territory. The windows at the docks that were in use were frosted or blacked out. Only the empty ones had clear windows, which also explained the winding corridors; none of those windows showed a ship in dock.

I reached the Lava Grill with its red and orange décor and a mix of tourists trying to get used to this strange place and ship's crews waiting to come or go. It served wonderful pulled pork garnished with pineapple, but their cookies were even better.

By then, I was starting to *feel* like a freelancer again.

Beyond the grill were shops selling contraband, or what was contraband elsewhere, a drug shop selling hallucinogens, a tech shop with hacking hardware and software, and a brothel boasting zero-g rooms with backdrops of a hundred planets.

When I reached the vaulted walkway between the spaceport and the domed city of Puerto Fronterizo, I stepped to the side and watched. I'd spent almost five years flying in and out of here in my exile. After this trip, I doubted I'd be back, although I didn't know what I *would* do. I still didn't have a home, other than *Hiram's Revenge*. Conrad Maeda, my old boss at Pauley Spaceways Special Projects, would probably hire me back, but that wasn't for me. Maybe some small engineering firm, but I'd miss flying *Hiram's Revenge*. It was also time for me to move out of Kaia's place. It had been nice living with my chatterbox college roommate again for a few months, but I needed to find or make my *own* home.

Just the thought created a hollowness in my chest and a darkness in my soul. I'd gotten away from the bastards who'd created me, at least mostly. But how did one go about making a home? A life? Go back and steal Hiram from his wife? That just seemed wrong.

With a shake of the head, I pushed off and headed through the vaulted corridor and into Puerto Fronterizo, now showing pyramids from Chichén Itzá in Mexico on the walls between the windows.

When I reached the end of the tunnel, I turned left at the first cross street, walking past the little shops that sold stolen software and cleaning robots, and others selling boring clothes or groceries.

I stepped up to the counter at Marta's empanada place and leaned on it. I did not recognize the young woman ready to take my order.

Smiling, I held up three fingers. "Today's special, tres, and a horchata. I'm Deuce, and I'd like to talk to Marta."

She served me the empanadas and drink with a smile and went to the back to find Marta.

When Marta stepped out into the restaurant and saw me, she rushed around the counter and gave me a hug. "Deuce! We thought you were dead!"

I held her at arm's length. "No, just learning how to end my exile. Still not sure I've figured it out."

Someone called out, "Burgundy!"

I ignored him. No one knew that name here. Marta looked and scowled, not pleased with what she saw.

The same voice, somewhat quieter, said, "Deuce! I need you."

Furious, I turned, sluggish and calculated to annoy. I found Admiral Jackson, retired, striding toward me with four men in tow, all looking like hired muscle. Jackson had been my sister Brandy's commanding officer in the Nova Roman war, and my workout partner or something like that at the Clark Academy. What the hell was *he* doing here? And how dare he use my real name! Marta would figure it out for sure.

One of Jackson's thugs had a big, black mustache. Another had a black eye. The third had long blond hair, and the fourth was a woman who looked like a bodybuilder. What a motley crew.

Jackson stepped right up to Marta and me. "Walk with me."

I rolled my eyes or Marta, then shook my head and walked down the road with Jackson.

Once out of earshot from Marta, Jackson pitched his voice low. "I'm staging a rescue, and I need to hire a pilot for the escape. I was just headed to the Abogada, but this job is made for you."

I stopped and put hands on hips. "Then my price just tripled."

Jackson raised an eyebrow, then nodded with a grin. "Done."

He held out a hand for me to shake.

Oh, hell. If he would do that without a thought, this was dangerous and difficult. But I hadn't said quintuple, which I apparently should have. He always seemed like he knew more than he was letting on. Still, he had helped me back at the Clark Academy and had been a friend of my sister Brandy for years. I wasn't sure I owed him anything, but he was an old friend.

I shook his hand, and we started off. I'd intended to go get a drink from Ramon, the bartender at the Abogada. I turned to wave at Marta. "Tell Ramon and the gang at the Abogada that I'm still alive." I gave Jackson a glance. "For now."

She winked at me, but she looked worried. "I will."

I fell in beside Jackson and pitched my voice low. "What the hell?"

He snorted. "Frankly, I was lucky you were here. I've been living here a few months and got word a spy was kidnapped. We need to get him back."

Why did I think luck had nothing to do with it? And what did a retired admiral have to do with spies? Still, I used my bracer to send a quick message to Earl. "Get the *Revenge* ready to fly. Leaving sooner than expected."

And suddenly, without trying, I was in deep, deeper than I wanted or needed. "That brings up nineteen more questions. Where are we flying?"

He hesitated. "Thurman."

I hadn't planned to go back to my home planet, but I didn't have anywhere else to go either. Still, this sounded less and less good. I shook my head as we walked. "I should have asked for ten times my rate."

Jackson laughed.

When we reached the main road, we turned away from the spaceport, deeper into Puerto Fronterizo.

As we walked, a realization struck me. In other places, like Beijing, you could tell the good and bad neighborhoods by the shabbiness of the houses and how well places were maintained, even if humble. Not in a place like Angel's Planet. Nothing here was more than twenty years old, most less than ten. And all of it had been constructed with the same giant printers, using the same raw materials. All the buildings had charcoal gray walls with blue and orange highlights.

Near the center of town, Jackson led us left again, into a neighborhood I did not know. The buildings rose two or three stories above us, making a gray canyon with shops below and apartments above, all with windows, some with balconies. The canyons grew tighter and darker when Jackson cut through an alleyway. No windows broke the walls there, just a few emergency doors above us that would extrude their own stairs or ladders if needed.

At last, the alley expanded into a little open-air market that had food and recreational drugs sold side-by-side, and which opened to a normal street on the far side. The only similar market I'd been to sold clothes and hacking tools.

Here, tourists and locals lounged on chairs eating and getting
high.

We crossed the market, weaving between chairs and
vendor's carts, and stopped at the far by the next street.
There, Jackson turned to face all of us. "He's in room three-
seventeen in that hotel across the street." He pointed at
Mustache thug. "Get to the roof, make sure they don't have
anyone up there. Then let us know if anyone else comes in."

Mustache stroked his facial hair, tapped his ear, and
headed out, turning left, and going up the street a bit before
crossing.

Jackson turned back with a grin. "I'm hungry. Let's get
something to eat."

We went back and got some kabobs and watched people
getting high. The food-cart vendor had spiced the vat-grown
meat well. I savored every bite.

It only took a few minutes before Jackson cocked his
head. "Scout on the roof eliminated. Now we walk in the front
door like we belong."

That's when I noticed they all had earbuds. Belatedly, I
dashed after Jackson and his thugs as they crossed the
street.

I elbowed him. "When do I get an earbud?"

Jackson ignored me.

Walking into the hotel lobby was like walking into a
nudist beach in San Tropez. The room had a gorgeous cove
displayed on three walls, with beach chairs and real sand
trickling onto the floors. On those lounge chairs reclined four
men and three women, all rather naked and available for
various services. A massage—a real one for stiff muscles—
sounded good about now. Of course, I didn't buy services
when I could afford to buy the whole brothel. If I wanted to.

Jackson didn't even pause, though his thugs took some
long looks.

There was an elevator in the hallway off the main lobby,
but Jackson trotted up the stairs next to it. The stairway was
utilitarian, printed like the exterior walls but with slip-proof
treads added. Again, I brought up the rear.

By the time I reached the third floor, the others had
already gone out into the hall and the metal door was

swinging shut. I slipped through into a corridor with black carpet speckled with the same blues as the grays walls. Ten meters down, I saw Jackson and hairy thug flanking the near side of the door for three-seventeen, with bodybuilder and shiner standing on the other side. None of them stood directly in front of the opening.

I warmed up my plasma pistol.

Hairy, whose locks made me jealous, pulled out a small electronic device. I arrived just as Jackson reached over to knock.

Someone answered from inside. Jackson spoke with a thick accent. Then four shots punched through the door.

Hairy held his device to the lock. The door popped open. Shiner drew a firearm, pushed the door open, and dove in. The wall on the far side told me the room extended my direction.

Shots came at a sharp angle. From someone standing beside the door. The thugs fired back.

If the bad guy was standing beside the door, he'd be right by me. I turned and fired through the wall. The plasma blasted through the thin printed internal wall.

Then I hit the carpet. Shots flew out the hole I'd made. Hairy and Bodybuilder launched through the door. Two shots and a couple thuds followed.

One of the thugs called, "All clear!"

Jackson and I went in. A regular hotel room with smart walls, the ceiling set to mirror and the walls to some park. The bed had hooks designed for tying up guests. Shiner-thug was on the ground, writhing in pain. Two strangers lay on the carpet, one bleeding, one moaning. A woman lay tied to the bed.

Assuming the one on the bed was the one we'd come to rescue, I dashed over and untied her.

She sat up, rubbing her wrists. "Who the hell are you idiots?"

I leaned close so the thugs wouldn't hear. "That's Admiral Jackson, who commanded the 14th in the war."

At that moment, Jackson, who'd knelt to put a pressure bandage on Shiner's wound, cocked his head. "We have visitors." Then he pointed at Hairy. "You change clothes with her. The three of you go to the bus terminal and buy tickets for Volcan Diablo. Then go to the women's room and change clothes again. Hurry!"

The woman on the bed had started to strip already. She showed no modesty at all.

Hairy scowled until Jackson offered to double his pay. Then he stripped and donned the woman's clothes.

The woman in thug clothing stopped to search through the pants of her bleeding captor to retrieve a data crystal, which she stuffed into her own pants. "Let's go."

Jackson sent Hairy and Bodybuilder dragging the wounded Shiner to the elevator. The rest of us went down the stairs. At the bottom, Jackson peeked out the door, then waited. At last, he signaled us, and we trooped out, back through the lobby and out under the dome.

We met Mustache back in the little market area, and headed out in a diamond, Mustache out front and our quarry in back, pretending to be a bodyguard. I noticed she did a good job checking our surroundings.

At last, we reached the vaulted passage back to the spaceport. Then I felt a little safer, though this was a place we had to go, so someone might set an ambush here.

I stepped a little closer to Jackson in our diamond formation. "What the hell is this?"

"She's a spy with important information the Romans don't want the Council of Planets to get. Those guys who had her were hired to kidnap her on Tanterra, which has some laws the Romans didn't want to openly cross."

It made sense for them to bring a kidnap victim here to Angel's Planet, since no one here would care. It was the sort of thing Angel himself made sure no one cared about, he owned the whole planet. And I could get her to Thurman or even Earth faster than anyone but a courier.

When I wondered what I would do now that I had money, this hadn't been one of the choices.

We made it out of the tunnel into the terminal building. No ambush.

Still, I guided Mustache past the spaceport shops, around to the Lava Grill and through the winding corridors way out to the end. This time I walked right past the windows that looked out over the Precipice and the roiling sky.

Earl's shop was the last door in the spaceport, where the corridor ended. Nothing lay beyond. From the windows, you could also see the shop extending out over the precipice. The floor there tilted down to let ships in and out. Since *Hiram's Revenge* was inside, Earl had given me access. The door had a sign that read *Earl Cristo, Starship Mechanic.*

I'd spent weeks with Earl building new Lu Space controls for *Hiram's Revenge* and selling the invention to Pauley Spaceways, and I'd yet to see any sign of a personality. His robot dog, Roberre, who could be playful, tender, and imposing had more personality.

The door recognized me, so I pulled it open and held it for Mustache.

We trooped into the front office, a room with smooth surfaces, a counter, and a door, nothing else. The door to the shop stood open and inviting. Since no one was in the front office, we headed on into the shop. I wondered where Roberre was. Usually, he met strangers right at the door.

Someone moved beside the doorway. A shot rang out.